Nu

Michael Atkinson

For Catrina,

To quote Effie Trinket,
"May the odds be
ever in your favor!"
 – Michael Atkinson

Copyright @2013 by Michael Atkinson
All rights reserved.
No part of this publication may be reproduced or transmitted in any form or by any means without prior permission from the author.

To Madeline Smith, aka "Gaseous Girl". This novel isn't about you, unfortunately, but the next one is. And you do get a brief mention in one chapter. So glad your relationship with the Wombat is working out, by the way. I had worried.

Acknowledgements

First, thanks so much to Julia Brinkworth, who served as a beta reader for this story, and caught several things I'd missed, such as random misspellings, and the final disposition of the Sporksaber. Secondly, thanks to Taylor Troncin, who created the front cover picture of the good captain. As the song goes, one can get by with a little bit of help from one's friends. Any continuity or grammar errors that remain in the story are entirely my own.

Prologue

This is not Catrina's story. She does have one, make no mistake, and it's very lovely; it involves her quest to find Mlrning (the Shovel of Thor!), not to mention time travel, Vikings and a morosely aristocratic penguin. But that story, fascinating as it may be, is not the one being told here. That being the case, one might wonder why Catrina was walking down the streets of Edison City, her boots squelching in slush left over from a recent snow shower, her left hand casually gripping the hilt of her Sporksaber. Catrina ought to have known that this wasn't her tale, but no one had ever explained to her how impolite it was to interrupt someone else's story. Besides, she was bored. Her quest to find Mlrning (the Shovel of Thor!) hadn't quite gotten started yet, and she wanted something to do. That explained why she was meandering down the sidewalk, glancing in store windows and generally finding nothing of interest. Nothing free, anyway, and as Catrina had just come in from the 12th century she had a deplorable lack of 21st century currency.

She was still having difficulty getting used to the modern world. Everything was so noisy and bright, with neon signs everywhere, sirens blaring and people bustling around or yelling into their cell phones. Catrina hadn't been introduced to cell phone technology yet; as a result, she had gotten the mistaken impression that the modern world was full of odd people who spent most of their time talking to themselves. They also spent an inordinate amount of time talking about angry birds and tweets, which was a puzzlement to Catrina since she hadn't seen any birds in the city except for a pigeon doing its business on a statue.

This sight didn't exactly endear Catrina to the metropolis, and she had just about decided to give up and try to find her way back to her own time period, when all at once she came upon a bookstore. It was then that a brilliant idea hit her.

Catrina had known for some time that she wasn't a real person, that she was instead a fictional character sprung from her author's imagination. She'd even come to accept this in some way, although she was somewhat distressed by her author's tendency to kill her off and then resurrect her. After about the fifth or sixth death, it began to get wearisome. At any rate, since she was a fictional character, that meant she had to be in a book. And here she was outside a bookstore. Was it possible...?

She wasted no time in darting inside. Then she paused. The bookstore was a lot bigger then she'd suspected. Where might her adventures be? Obviously the nonfiction section was out, as were the sections of travel guides and calendars. Catrina browsed through the shelves, her brow furrowing in confusion. She'd kissed Perry a time or two, and in fact she was now married to him, unless her author had rewritten her backstory without her knowing. Perhaps she'd gotten put in the Romance section? Catrina flipped through the first cheap paperback she found, just to see if it might be something like what she experienced. At about page 57, her eyes grew wide as dinner plates and her face went red as the blade of her Sporksaber. She most certainly hadn't experienced *that*. Catrina dropped the paperback like it was a spider that should be stepped on, and moved quickly to the Mystery section. Some things just didn't bear reading about.

The Mystery section yielded no joy, and neither did the children's shelves. Catrina didn't think having a shoulder angel put one in the Christian Fiction category, and she skipped right over Horror. She had just about given up her search when she came upon Fantasy and Sci-Fi. Catrina's eyes lit, and her trademark half-smile slid slowly on her face. There it was, in black and white, her very own name. *Catrina in Space*. True, it wasn't the biggest book on the shelf, nor the shiniest, but it was her story and it was wonderful.

Reverently she took it from the shelf, gazing in awe upon the shiny cover. She had no way of knowing that the stars were only a stock photo provided by the publishing company. Instead, Catrina assumed that the author had drawn the picture himself. "Oh my..." she breathed, her heart tripping in excitement. She had to buy it, to read what the author said about her. Had she been written properly? She had to know! But there was the problem again: she didn't have a dime of 21st-century money. Or did she? Catrina checked her pockets: lint, figurine of a manatee, more lint...nothing. She considered. Perhaps this was one of the type of booksellers who would give a book away if the buyer had read it twice, and said it was her favorite, and it was hers because she liked it so much. She tentatively approached the counter. "Er, I don't suppose..."

"Hi!" the cashier said perkily. "Do you have a member's card with us today?"

"I don't think I-"

"It has all sorts of benefits! A 15 percent discount on any book you buy in-store, and you get emails about new discounts and pre-release offers!"

"Maybe some-"

"The form's super easy to fill out! And it's only 12.95 the first time, ten to renew! It's a great opportunity!"

"Look, I just-"

"And you get a free pen with our logo! Try it!" The cashier slid the pen merrily across the countertop, along with the form. Catrina glanced at it, noting that it asked for such incomprehensible things as her zip code and email address. Not being overly familiar with the United States Postal Service, Catrina had little idea what a zip code might be.

Finally she gave up, and slid the form politely back. "I actually don't have any of your timeline's money on me right now," she explained. "I was wondering if I could take this book anyway; it's got me in it, you see."

The cashier's nose scrunched in confusion. "But...that's from our Fantasy section. You're a real person. The book can't have you in it."

Catrina suddenly realized that the cashier hadn't broken through the glass fourth wall, so to speak, and had no idea that she wasn't a real person either. She thoughtfully decided not to shatter the girl's existence. "What I meant was, I wrote it."

The cashier was even more confused. "But...the author's a guy. You're not."

Catrina honestly hadn't noticed that yet; she was somewhat relieved, as she had never been entirely sure what the gender of her author was. "Yes. Well. I helped with the...erm, pictures."

"Oh..." the cashier said, still bewildered. "Well....you didn't get that off the promotional table, did you?"

Catrina glanced around, and saw a small table near the door lined with older-looking books, with a small cardboard sign on it that said "Free". Apparently the store was doing this in the hopes that their customers would think kindly of them and come back for books that actually required payment. So far it wasn't going wonderfully well, as the only books the store was giving away were the ones that no one wanted to read anyway. This little lesson in economics escaped Catrina entirely; she'd never cared much for the maths. She was now facing an ethical dilemma, though; she hadn't pulled her book off the promotional table, but she couldn't get it unless she said she had. "Not exactly," she dithered, "...but maybe there's another copy that is on the table. Let me go check."

"You do that," the relieved cashier said, secretly hoping that this unusual customer wouldn't return until after her shift.

Catrina went over to the promotional table and examined the piles of books. Most of them didn't seem interesting at all, and none of them were her own story. Then, near the bottom of the last pile, she found a worn copy of another book with her author's name on it. Catrina smiled. This might be even better. She knew her own story already anyway, she'd lived it. But if she could see what else her author had done, maybe she could finally come to understand her own world, like why she kept getting killed off. She took the story from the table and sought out a comfortable chair in the bookstore's attached coffee shop. There, with her free logo-emblazoned pen in hand, she began reading carefully through the pages, making neat comments throughout. "Well," she thought, "This is...interesting...."

Chapter One

Night had fallen in the city. Marsha knew she was terribly late, and she really shouldn't be walking through the dimly lit streets alone, but she was in a hurry to get home. Besides, Edison City was a city of superheroes now, and things like muggings just didn't happen much anymore. Most muggers had moved away to small rural towns, as the caped crusaders never seemed to bother much with protecting small rural towns, except for that one over in Illinois[1]. What Marsha had forgotten was that although Edison City was a city of superheroes, it was also a city of supervillains. And while most supervillains tended to develop grandiose plans involving blimps or powerful bombs or mass hostage situations, some of them were more prosaic. Like, the Rogue Jaywalker, for example, who now lurched out of a doorway and into her path.

"Right," he said in a quick, scared voice, "gimme all your money! Now!"

"Oh dear," Marsha said. "I don't actually have, like, cash on me?"

---

[1] Hi there, loyal readers. This is Catrina. Look, I don't just read books, okay? I gotta take notes. Explain things. I'm sure the author's sweet and all, but he really doesn't have a clue about how Edison City works. He hasn't even named all his characters yet, as of this writing. So I've got to step in. Again. Sigh. At any rate, I thought I would point out here that the small town he's referring to is not the one you're thinking of, the one that's in Kansas. That would totally be a copyright violation and would be wrong. You will notice that this is a small town that's in another state altogether. It's called Pocaville. Their main superhero is the Sneeze. That's her power. Really, really bad allergies. It's sad.

"You got credit cards, right?"

"Yeah, but you know I'll cancel them as soon as I get home. Standard procedure nowadays. You won't be able to do much with them."

The Rogue Jaywalker hesitated. "Maybe a gift card to a nice restaurant somewhere?"

"Nope."

"A keychain that gets you a free drink at the gas station?"

"Used it. Lost it."

"...a Chuck-E-Cheese token?"

"I don't have kids."

The Rogue Jaywalker sighed. "Ya might as well give me the credit cards anyway. Maybe I can use 'em real quick before you cancel." All this time a thought had been slowly taking shape in his mind; finally, it connected. "Or maybe...since I'm holding the deadly weapon here, I could just shoot you and then you wouldn't be able to cancel anything."

"Oh. Yes. Well....but that would be..." Marsha scrambled for something to say. "That would be bad!"

An evil smile spread across the Rogue Jaywalker's face. "Lady, I'm a supervillain. Bad's what I do."

She couldn't argue with that logic. With a sigh, Marsha surrendered to the inevitable, and prepared herself to give the usual scream of terror that people in her situation gave right before the villain shot them. She'd actually been practicing her dying screams of late, and had even been working with a vocal coach; one could never be too prepared in Edison City. But now it looked like she would never have the chance to work with that coach at all. Marsha opened her mouth to scream as the Rogue

Jaywalker leveled his gun at her. Instead of a scream, however, what she heard was a sudden thunderclap, like a jet plane blasting overhead during an airshow. The Rogue Jaywalker looked quizzically at her, almost as if he thought she'd made the noise herself. Then it suddenly dawned on him what the sound really meant. His eyes widened in fear and he moved to hide the gun he was holding. It was too late.

A blur of red and white flashed overhead, landing with a smash in the alleyway. Boots swept out in a mighty roundhouse kick, and the Rogue Jaywalker himself hurtled back into a nearby dumpster. Marsha's mouth fell open. She knew this hero well. He'd even saved her once before, during one of the city's many apocalypses.
"You're...Captain Happily Married!"

The good captain swept back his white cape and made a polite bow. "Are you unharmed?"

"Oh, yes, he hadn't gotten around to firing yet," Marsha said.

"Very good!" said Captain Happily Married. "I hope this little experience wouldn't discourage you from walking through alleyways; statistically speaking it's much more likely that you would be mauled by wild marmosets[2]!"

Marsha actually had a friend who'd been mauled by wild marmosets; she was about to point this out when

---

[2] Catrina again. I don't know where he's getting his statistics. Or even what the margin of error is. He may have looked this up on Wikipedia, for all I know. Anyway, if anyone reading this is doing a study comparing alleyway muggings to marmoset maulings, I would advise you to do your own research. It's generally a poor idea to take statistical advice from a guy who flies around in tights, even if he can hurl a unity candle with deadly accuracy.

Captain Happily Married blasted off and soared away into the night sky. She sighed, and pulled out her phone to put in a call to the police. It was, for her, just another ordinary night in Edison City.

Above the tall skyscrapers, the captain cruised pleasantly, his cape billowing out behind him. So far the night's patrol had gone splendidly. He had saved four civilians from attempted muggings, prevented a high-speed train from crashing, foiled Thunderdomestic's latest evil plot to take over the city's Wal-Marts, and put out a fire in a burning apartment building, while saving everyone inside and preserving the building's structural integrity. The captain decided to make one more sweep of the city and then turn in. Something was bothering him, though, a slight suspicion that he had forgotten something. Was it his finely tuned Matri-Senses?"

It was at that moment that his communicator chirped in his utility belt. "Captain Happily Married," he responded.

"Hey, dear. You were going to pick up some milk from the store, right?"

Ah. That was it. "Right, of course I was. Am. I was on the way only five minutes ago, when I had to save a poor innocent bystander from the Rogue Jaywalker!"

"Naturally. Oh, could you hold on a sec?"

He heard a rustle, and then a series of *whaps* and *thuds*, followed by a loud *whoompf*. The captain checked his watch for the date; he hadn't thought it was his wife's patrol night as well. He'd have to check the calendar when he got home.

"Sorry," she said, coming back on the line, "Commander Cockroach . You know how he is."

"Commander Cockroach! What new villainy has he unleashed?"

"Dear, could you turn down the monologue voice? It's just me, you know."

"Oh, yes, of course. Sorry about that. So do you need any help, or..."

Another *whoompf* resounded in the background. "No, I got this. Oh, you'll probably get home before I do, so you'll need to make sure Hope gets her check; I left it in the kitchen."

Captain Happily Married's eyes narrowed, in the look he usually gave supervillains planning to set off the explosive device tied to the train tracks. "I thought Meg was going to watch the kids next patrol. She *said* she would, didn't she? I distinctly remember us having this discussion!"

"Yes, well, she didn't show, and I couldn't get hold of her on her phone, so..."

"This..." the captain rumbled, "is becoming a problem. She is becoming increasingly unreliable!"

"Dear," she replied calmly, "I don't think now is the right time to have this discussion."

"Because you think that we can't work through our difficulties like reasonable people, and address this problem like adults?"

"No, because there's a robot with laser eyes trying to blow up my left arm, and I've used up my last exploding soccer ball."

The captain hesitated in midflight. "You sure you're okay, Tasha?"

"Yeah, just need to...hang on..." he heard a loud explosion, and static burst over the phone. It cleared up in a second, though, and then he heard her voice again. "He's getting smarter. The robot had protective lead shielding over his interface port. Took me longer than usual to 'path in. But that was the last one. I already got the big guy, so I just need to mop up and then make another circle round the park. See you at home."

"Right," Captain Happily Married said. "See you there. And we do need to talk about this situation with Meg."

She sighed. "Of course we do. Bye."

The captain placed his communicator back in his utility belt and banked towards home. Then he banked again, remembered just in time that he was supposed to pick up milk from the store. He was Captain Happily Married, after all; he never forgot these sorts of things. Why, he even always remembered their anniversary date[3]! With that cheery thought in mind, the good captain swept away into the night, cape streaming heroically behind him.

What he didn't see, down on the streets below, was a woman in a trench coat staring up at him through powerful binoculars. The trench coat might have made her more inconspicuous had it not been solid white, and embroidered with colorful unicorns and rainbows. Having inexplicably escaped the notice of Captain Happily Married, she packed away her binoculars and slipped into an alleyway; not only were they great for muggings, they were also stellar for secretive communications. She pulled out a

---

[3] Suuuuure he does.

cell phone and dialed carefully; this was absolutely not the time to get a wrong number. "Sir?" she said in a whisper a few degrees too loud. "Candystriper reporting in. You were totally right, sir. They're having difficulties with their oldest daughter. They almost had an argument!"

"Almost. And what, exactly, do you mean by almost?"

Candystriper blinked. "Well....they didn't fight exactly..."

"Then what's the point? I knew they were having problems with Meg already. What is critical is whether their problems have reached the level of a serious family crisis! And so far they haven't, because you tell me that they only *almost* had an argument! Did they actually *do* anything or just *almost* do it?"

"Um..." Candystriper stammered. "Well...th-they had to hire a babysitter? For their kids. Because Meg was supposed to do it and she didn't. This isn't the first time either. I had a babysitter when I was a wee little minion, you know. True story. At least....I think I did....it may have been in a prior life. No...two prior lives ago. The one where I was reincarnated as a flower child in Santa Monica. Not this one."

"Candystriper, you're digressing again. Back on point, they hired a babysitter. Wonderful. Well, now my plan is certain to succeed, now that I know they had to hire a babysitter just like half the other families in America. This is truly astounding news."

Candystriper, not being the most mentally together of minions, took this literally. "I'm so relieved you think so, sir!"

A frustrated sigh. "That was sarcasm. This isn't good news at all. I will need to intensify other elements of our plan sooner than I had anticipated. Their marriage is more durable than expected!"

"Sir," Candystriper asked, not unreasonably, "couldn't you just kill them off now? I know a guy, he's got this Kaboominator, see, and it's guaranteed to blow up even the capes with super-strength, and-"

"Candystriper?"

"Yes, sir?"

"Shut up."

The phone went dead. She gaped at it for a minute, then disconsolately tucked it away. "I still don't see why he doesn't just kill 'em off now..." she mumbled to herself. But then, that was why she was a lowly minion, and her boss wasn't. She just didn't understand these sorts of things[4].

Meanwhile, Captain Happily Married had dutifully picked up the milk from the grocery store, and was coming in for a landing on the neatly mown lawn of his home, an ordinary cookie-cutter two-story place on Citrus Street[5]. The house, he noted with some relief, looked undamaged;

---

[4] I don't either. Because the Kaboominator seems like a really good idea. I know I shouldn't be rooting for the villain here, but I very much want to see the Kaboominator in action. Maybe it'll show up later?

[5] You're probably wondering at this point exactly *how* the good captain got the milk; did he change into his secret identity, pick it up, change back, and fly away? Well, no, apparently he carries a bit of cash in his utility belt, and grocery store people in Edison City are entirely used to seeing superheroes fly in and buy stuff. Comes of living in a superhero town, I expect.

he had always worried about that ever since he'd heard about the Great Babysitter Disaster of '14, where Atomica had inadvertently engaged a civilian sitter to watch her pyrokinetic child. The resulting disaster had made the nightly news and spawned a hundred Internet memes, and since then superheroes had made sure only to call upon the small but capable cadre of superpowered babysitters.

The captain walked up to his front door without checking to see if anyone was looking; although he lived within the suburbs of the city, his house was at the end of a tree-lined cul-de-sac with only two other houses on their street, and he knew for a fact that both of them were occupied by other superhero families. He pulled out his key, but the door opened before he could unlock it; evidently Hope had seen him landing. She looked a bit frazzled. As did the five other Hopes standing behind her. Captain Happily Married wasn't fazed a bit. "Are the Twins in bed, then?"

"Yeah, finally," Hope said. "There's three more of me upstairs cleaning up. I gotta say, Captain, I'll be glad when they, like, get out of the terrible twos and get power control, y' know?"

"Indeed," the captain said, following her inside. "We had that same problem with Sauna before she learned."

Hope winced. "About that...she hasn't come out of her room. The whole time. I hope I didn't upset her?"

Captain Happily Married assured the concerned babysitter that she didn't; his daughter was probably just going through a phase. He didn't understand this sort of thing himself; Tasha was better at working with their daughter. It occurred to the captain that he'd hardly even *seen* Sauna since...well, her fifteenth birthday party, and that was five months ago, and she'd only shown up for a few moments before she'd melted the cake and left yelling that no one understood her. "Well....everyone else doing okay?"

Hope shrugged. "Well, Tamsin had a fight with Aaron 'cause he was power-experimenting and she was Frisbeeing and he accidentally shifted her back to human form right when she was flying over the trash can. They yelled a bit, but everyone calmed down eventually. Tamsin did her math work and went to bed half an hour ago; Aaron's still up, working on a song, I think. Caden's still up, too, but, then, that's normal for him. I wish I had his power, sometimes. Not having to sleep could be super useful."

The captain sighed. "Not as much as you'd think." They'd had discussions with Caden over this; Caden suffered sometimes from power envy. "Well, I do appreciate your work, protecting our children from peril while we patrol the city in search of villainy!"

He had drifted into his monologue voice again; Hope didn't seem to care. "No problem, Captain. I gotta head home, Intro to American Political Philosophy test tomorrow that I need to cram for. Didn't quite finish tonight."

"Ah. Yes, indeed. Good show; education is certainly a valuable part of our society!"

"Totally," she agreed, yawning. "'Night."

The Captain bid her farewell, and then bid farewell to all the Hope-clones trooping out behind her, and closed the door on them all. Only then did he remember that he hadn't given her the check Tasha had left; he headed for the kitchen to make sure she had gotten it. Evidently she had; the table was clear of everything except a ketchup stain on the tablecloth, and that had been there for two weeks. Fighting supervillains could, occasionally, get in the way of proper housekeeping, the captain reflected. He wondered if he should make an observation to Tasha, but prudently decided against it. He checked his watch and turned on the television; it was Monday night after all, and the Edison City Carbon Filaments were playing the Lewisville Slugs. It was supposed to be a really good game. The captain was particularly looking forward to this one; he had gotten into a fantasy football league with a few of the other superheroes he knew, and he'd been lucky enough to draft the Carbon Filament defense early on. He was playing Mr. Superlative this week, and Superlative's defense wasn't worth spit. He had a good offensive line, though, but his best wide receiver was on bye that week, which meant the Captain had a pretty fair chance of beating him[6].

Back out in the city, Tasha was finally making her way towards home. It had been a close thing, closer than she wanted to admit to Justin. "Winston," she said to the soccer ball resting next to her in the passenger seat of the Miraculous Minivan, "make a note about that protective shielding, would you? I want to know where Cockroach got that idea. He certainly didn't come up with it himself."

Winston beeped in acknowledgment, filing the note away in its capacious memory banks. An ordinary passer-by

---

[6] I don't pretend to understand fantasy football myself, so I'm not even going to try to explain what the captain's talking about here while he's doing his little inner monologue. All I know is that the fantasy part of it has nothing to do with elves or dragons. Very sad.

might have wondered exactly how a soccer ball had memory banks[7], but this was no ordinary soccer ball. This was a soccer ball crammed with nanobots and electric microchips and more fancy gadgets than a roomful of eccentric inventors could dream of, and thanks to a long-ago tour with the East Plazniki intelligence agency, the whole thing was keyed specially to Tasha's brain[8]. She had added a few devices herself, primarily juice-box holders and a neat little attachment that changed a diaper in seventeen seconds flat. With seven kids, two of whom were twins that had the ability to clone themselves, that one came in awfully handy.

Tasha rounded the last corner onto her street, powering down the Minivan's rocket thrusters and making sure the hydraulics had stabilized. She didn't want to wake up the neighbors, not that they weren't used to those sorts of things, but still, it wasn't polite.

Just as she turned into her driveway, Winston emitted a new beep which meant that she had an incoming call. Tasha checked the readout; it was Meg Atomic. Tasha sighed, wondering if she wanted to get into this right now with her errant oldest child. She briefly considered letting it go to voicemail, but then chided herself. She was Super Soccer Mom, after all, and this was exactly the sort of thing

---

[7] I was wondering that myself, actually.

[8] I don't expect the author will include a map in this thing; his drawing skills don't appear to progress much beyond stick figures and the Batman logo. At any rate, East Plaznik is, according to my research, somewhere in Eastern Europe. Right next to Suzistan. You can't miss it.

she was supposed to do. "Patch it through, Winston," she said, sighing.

Winston beeped again, and one of the dark patches on the soccer ball flipped around into a speaker. Meg's voice rasped through. "Hey, Mom. Look, I wanted to apologize about tonight. I had-"

"Meg," Tasha said firmly. "I'm sure you had a good reason. But even so, you said that you would be here and you weren't. You knew we needed a full-powered super to look after the kids while we were on patrol. Sauna hasn't gotten her license yet, and Aaron's still on a permit. We needed you, and you weren't there. Thank heavens we could get Hope in time; if we couldn't, and something had happened..."

"Well, nothing did," Meg cut in. "And I do not need your guilt trip. I was going to call you, but Tempestuous attacked before I could. She plays havoc with cell phone reception, you know."

"Tempestuous? But she usually attacks near Tidal, clear across the country. Since when are you based in Tidal?"

"I was...visiting a friend. "

"Oh, Meg. You're not still seeing-"

"Do not start, Mom. Do *not* start. He has changed."

Tasha's hands clenched white on the steering wheel. "Meg, how can you say that? He blew up an entire pharmacy!"

"Last year. After he got everyone out. And it was going to be shut down anyway. And he wanted to make a political statement about-"

"I don't care *what* he wanted to make a political statement about!"

"Well, maybe you *should!*" Meg shot back. "He is the only one in this whole country who is even near the same intelligence quotient as I am, which means he is practically the only one with whom I can have a conversation! He is the only one who understands me on a truly philosophical level!"

"And he's a supervillain," Tasha said angrily. "He didn't care so much about innocent lives when he attacked the parade last Christmas."

"Ex-supervillain. You will recall that he *is* an ex-supervillain because he cooperated with the federal investigators and helped put the villain he was truly working for, Queenpin, behind bars. Multiple-lives sentences, remember? She would not have received that penalty had it not been for him."

"And look what he got out of it. They let him walk free!"

"Precisely. Because they *trust* him."

"Well, I don't. And you shouldn't either!"

Meg's husky voice went calm. "Well, Mom, I am afraid you no longer have the right to make that call. I am going to keep seeing him. I do not much care whether you or Dad approves."

A sharp *click* echoed through Winston's speaker. Tasha laid her head down on the wheel. She hadn't met to get into *that* at all either. But to have her daughter dating the Malevolent Med-Student, of all people...why couldn't it have been the Wombat? She had hoped that relationship would work out. But then it had fallen apart, as relationships so often did with Meg. The Wombat seemed to be doing well now with Gaseous Girl, and Tasha didn't begrudge that at all, especially after that whole alternate-universe crisis. Still....she wished it had worked out. Because now Meg was heading for trouble, and the worst of it was that she was almost right about one thing. Tasha couldn't make that call now. All she could do was hope Meg would find her way somehow, before something really disastrous happened. And if it did, Tasha would be there for her. Because she was Super Soccer Mom, and that was what she did[9].

What she didn't do was tell the captain about this latest wrinkle in the Meg Situation. Tasha didn't want to worry him with the news that his oldest girl was seriously interested in a supervillain; she could only imagine his reaction. Right now all he knew was that Meg wasn't as reliable as she used to be; he would ponder that and possibly deliver a monologue about it, but hopefully Meg would get herself straightened out before too long and the whole thing would blow over. Besides, she knew what he would do if she told him; he would fly right over to Tidal and wallop the living daylights out of the Malevolent Med-Student, and that would probably not go over well with the civilian authorities. The Malevolent Med-Student hadn't doing anything violent, that she knew of since his release. For one second Tasha wondered. What if he had truly reformed?

With that troubling thought in mind, she left the Miraculous Minivan and headed inside. She could hear the television going in the living room; of course, it was

---

[9] *sniff*. I'm sorry, I've gotten allergies all of a sudden. I thought this was supposed to be a superhero parody. What's with the family drama all of a sudden? What do you think this is, *Full House*? Where's the sentimental clarinet music when you need it? Honestly.

Monday night, which meant football. With a sigh, Tasha pasted a smile on her face and went to ask the captain who was winning, and how that was affecting his fantasy team.

Chapter Two

Caden was bored. He got bored fairly frequently, especially when it came to the wee hours of the morning when everyone else would be asleep. Caden wondered sometimes what that must be like, going unconscious for hours on end. He'd asked his parents, and once or twice his siblings about it, but their answers had never satisfied him. The trouble with sleeping, it seemed, was that one could never be awake to analyze it. Caden had given up years ago, and decided to take up a hobby instead. Then he had discovered the Internet.

His favorite game was *Squoosh the Sara*. This involved infiltrating an evil empire dominated by a mutant pink hedgehog of gigantic size named Sara, who led an army of snarling hedgehog clones, which you had to squoosh with a titanium spork one received at the start of the game. If you successfully squooshed all the hedgehog clones and their robo-bunny allies, and recovered the treasure from the Secret Skittle Hills, and saved Princess Larkspur from the Hidden Shrine of the Cerulean Mollusk, you received access to Level Nine. Level Nine meant you had to face Sara herself[10].

Very few players had ever gotten all the way to Level Nine. Caden had done it twelve times. Not only that,

---

[10] I really want to play this game now. I could squoosh Sara in a heartbeat. I mean, I do have a Sporksaber, that's got to be better than a mere metal spork, even if it is made out of titanium. Sadly, though, for anyone reading this, I don't think *Squoosh the Sara* is sold in stores at the present time. Oh, and if any of you are computer programmers, my author might want to have a word with you.

but he held far away the game's highest score. He was something of a legend in the game's online community. Players who could work themselves into Ca1742's guild considered themselves honored beyond their wildest dreams, and those who were rejected often broke down in tears. Caden was considering, on that quiet Tuesday morning, whether to start a thirteenth run at the game; true, he'd already run through the possible ways to defeat Sara, but maybe there was one more way he hadn't worked out yet. Still...he had to admit, the whole thing was growing tiresome. You could only squoosh Sara so many times. But if he stepped back from the game, what else was he supposed to do?

It was while he was pondering this troubling question that his alarm clock rang. Caden didn't keep an alarm clock for himself, no point, really. But it helped to keep him on track, and besides, he had some time ago assigned himself the task of waking everyone else up. He was awake already anyway; he might as well. Caden slid back from his computer and padded into the hall.

His first stop was Tamsin's room; he usually started with her, mainly because she could then go into Sauna's room and wake her. Caden had never been quite comfortable with Sauna; she was always so moody. Not to mention, if you didn't wake her up delicately enough, she might very well lose control and set your hair on fire. Better that Tamsin should do it; she'd gotten to where she could Frisbee-shift as a reflex, thus avoiding the whole fire problem. Caden envied her for that, but then he envied all his siblings with real useful powers. All he could do was stay up late. What possible help could that be?

He poked his head around Tamsin's door. "Hey," he said quietly. "Time to get up."

She muttered something unintelligible and turned over. Caden felt for the light switch and flicked it on, whereupon Tamsin jerked awake, gasping in fright and Frisbeeing automatically. She shifted back when she realized what had happened, and then flung a pillow at her brother, who quickly backpedaled into the hallway. Starting with Tamsin was risky, he had to admit, but Sauna was riskier. Caden missed Meg Atomic sometimes; she had developed full power control far earlier than anyone else, and had always been nice to him.

She flung the door open and glowered at him from her purple Belle-embroidered pajamas. "Twerp," she said. "I was totally almost awake. You coulda, like, not turned the light on."

"Sorry," Caden apologized. "Would you please go wake Sauna now?"

"Whatevs," she said, waving dismissively at him and pushing past towards Sauna's room. Caleb headed down the hall towards Aaron and the Twins; behind him he heard Tamsin banging on the door and yelling. He, personally, would not have chosen that particular method of waking someone with Sauna's particular abilities, but then he couldn't turn into a nigh-indestructible Frisbee.

Caden tapped on Aaron's door, noting that his older brother had changed his poster again. He had some sports star up there; now it seemed to be another musician. Caden had never been much into Aaron's taste in music; he tended towards classical rather than rock. At any rate, he heard Aaron shuffling behind the door, and then a tousled head emerged. "Yeah."

"It's-"

"Yeah. I got it. Thanks. See ya." The door closed.

Aaron had never been much for conversation. Of course, he generated more than Sauna; at least he made an effort, whereas sometimes whole days would go by with Caden never even laying an eye on her.

The Twins he generally left to his mother, assuming they were still asleep when he got to them. Judging by the rattling sounds and shrieking he heard from the brightly decorated room they shared, he guessed they'd already started the day. Caden opened the door and peeked in; as usual the room was crawling with Jamies and Jeremys, and he could never tell which was which, let alone which were originals and which were clones. Yet another reason why he usually left that to his mother. Speaking of which, Caden headed downstairs, not without a wistful look at the tidy guest room that had once been Meg Atomic's. She hadn't been home for several years, not since she'd graduated college, but he still missed her.

As he approached the stairs leading to the ground floor, Tamsin nearly bowled him over. "Dude, you'd better not bother Sauna today," she advised breathlessly. "She's totally flipped. She almost burnt my PJs!"

"When would ever be a good day to bother Sauna?" Caden wanted to know.

Tamsin considered. "Um....probably, like, never. Also I think she's eating those super super spicy peppers in there again. I could smell 'em. I don't know how she does that. She doesn't even drink milk to cool down!"

"Side effect of her power," Caden started to explain. "She can-" But Tamsin had dashed off downstairs again, evidently in search of breakfast[11]. Caden sighed. She never listened to his explanations, and then she kept asking questions which she would've known the answers to had she listened. Meg had generally listened. And so did his mom, whom he could now see at the foot of the stairs.

"Twins up yet?" she asked.

"Yep. Don't know who's who, though."

"Some days I don't either," Tasha admitted laughingly, giving his brown hair a motherly tousle. Caden was getting to the point where he didn't care for that so much, but he tolerated it for now. She passed by, Winston bobbing in her wake, and went to see about corralling her duplicative offspring. She paused in the hallway and glanced back. "You remember today's the zoo, right?"

Caden had honestly forgotten. A sudden thought flashed across his mind. "Is...everyone coming?"

"Well, I don't know about Sauna, and Aaron's got work, but definitely Tamsin and the Twins..."

"I meant, um, is everyone coming from the group?"

Tasha smiled knowingly. "Oh. I was just talking to Audrey yesterday, and yes, Meredith is coming."

"Right. Not that I care, you know," Caden assured her. "I was only curious."

---

[11] To clarify, I think Sauna's power is that she can heat up the atmosphere around her, sometimes to almost pyromaniac levels, and also she has a really high tolerance for spicy foods and other hot things. She could touch a metal pan on a stove and not get burned. So she'll save a fortune on oven mitts, I expect.

Tasha was about to say something reassuring and Super-Soccer-Mommying, but unfortunately neither of them had noticed Tamsin coming back. Her eyes went wide with delight, and she immediately launched into a variation on the timeless classic, "Caden and Meredith, sitting in a tree, K-I-S-S-"

Caden fled, very much abashed, and Tasha delivered a stern look at her daughter. "Tamsin, you know you shouldn't-"

But she in her turn was interrupted as the Twins' door flew open and a mob of identical twin clones stampeded out, evidently in some improvised game of Tag in which everyone was It. "Winston!" Tasha yelled, and the soccer ball immediately chirped in reply, and emitted a high-pitched sound frequency that Tasha herself couldn't hear, but which she'd been told by her friends in East Plaznik could disrupt the telekinetic links that bonded the clones. Within seconds they all disappeared, leaving her with the original Jamie and Jeremy, who were still bubbling over with energy. Sometimes Tasha wondered how she would ever survive the week, much less the years that awaited her until the Twins learned to control their power. She was only grateful that they'd decided to stop with seven kids. At least, she was pretty sure they'd decided.

Sauna, as usual, elected not to go to the zoo; she slid a note out under her door explaining this decision, written in neat black ink and in the form of an elegantly constructed four-stanza free-verse poem in which she decried the whole system of zoology as being unfair to the animals, and went on to express how much she disliked their particular zoo, and the world in general, and concluded with a few lyrical thoughts on the possibility of rain. "A simple no would've sufficed," Tasha thought of saying, but decided not to. She was beginning to wonder if she would ever understand her daughter. Lately, she was beginning to wonder if she would ever *see* her daughter. At any rate, she couldn't spare much thought to this, as for the next hour she labored mightily in getting the Twins corralled and ready for their trip to the zoo. She then had to persuade Caden to go with them after all, which she only managed to do by making Tamsin apologize for teasing him. Tamsin dutifully apologized, though not very sincerely, and Caden reluctantly agreed to go with them. After more Herculean efforts from Tasha and a great many of Winston's wonderful gadgets, she finally got the Twins dressed, fed, and buckled up in their carseats, placed securely in the Miraculous Minivan. Tamsin and Caden climbed into the back seat, and after admonitions from Tasha to make sure everyone buckled up, and a Disney movie on the mini-player for the Twins, the Minivan's thrusters roared to life, and the minivan rocketed away towards the Edison City Zoo.

  Sauna watched them drive off, smoke trailing behind the super-powered vehicle. She felt a momentary flash of irritation that Tasha hadn't tried harder to get her to go with. But her mother never understood her anyways. No one understood her. It was all so unfair! The whole *world* was so-"

  She caught herself, just as steam began to billow up around her. Sauna closed her eyes tight, and concentrated on breathing slowly and thinking calming thoughts. She could get through this day, just like any other day. No one would know. All she had to do was stay away from irritation, remain calm, and everything would be fine. Sauna felt the temperature in her room drop again, and heard the confirming beep of the specially designed thermostat mounted on her wall. Slowly she opened her eyes again, and searched about for her ukulele. For some inexplicable reason, her ukulele music had proved the one thing that had kept her from losing it entirely. Sauna would've preferred a violin, but that would require her making a trip to the music store to buy one, and the last time she had done that she'd met this incredibly rude store assistant who obviously didn't know *one thing* about violins or music whatsoever and- she closed her eyes again, and began strumming quickly away at the ukulele. It was happening more often now. She had to do something about it, she knew. One couldn't play the ukulele forever[12].

Aaron left the house a few moments after the rest of the family had. He would've liked to go tearing off dramatically on his motorcycle, but unfortunately he didn't have one. What he had was a beat-up eggshell car he'd paid 2000 dollars for, and it was used, and he strongly suspected the dealer he'd bought it from wasn't entirely legit. It hadn't

---

[12] *giggle*. I'm sorry, I know she's having a moment here and I hate to interrupt, but really. "One couldn't play the ukulele forever?" If I had been writing this scene, I would've given the poor girl her violin. Now there's an instrument of passion, drama, seriousness. My author could've reworked that anecdote easily, but does he listen to me? Noooo. I'm only a poor lone fictional character; I get no respect. Anyway, I really think he only gave Sauna the ukulele just so he could see how often he could use ukulele in a sentence. Though it is a fun kind of word to say, I must admit. Like "smock". And "spleen". And "marina." Not to mention "wafting"...

even come with a CD player, it had a tape deck, and no one played cassette tapes anymore. Aaron had seen some of the newest cars where you didn't even need a CD player; you could just hook up your iPod or your Mp3 player. But cars like that required money, which Aaron didn't have much of. So he'd realistically assessed the situation, and started setting aside a few bucks a week to pay for a new radio. He hoped to have enough saved up by the end of the summer[13].

  He had left several minutes early, allowing plenty of time to navigate Edison City's often crowded streets and still make it to his shift at the Wally's Widgets factory on time. Aaron had to admit that, though he didn't use the tape deck much, at least the radio worked. He turned it on and flipped to the city's main news station, noting that it was almost time for the usual superhero activity report. Aaron was still on power-permit, but he looked forward to the day when he could don his own cape and join his parents in full-fledged city protection. He had already picked out his hero name. He hadn't quite worked out a uniform design yet; he was considering possibilities as a commercial played over the radio, in which two allegedly ordinary people discussed how they had saved so much money by switching to a certain brand of toilet cleaner, referencing the brand in an oddly specific way. Then came the dramatic theme that indicated the start of the radio station's Superhero Action Alert.

---

[13] Whoa. See, I thought my author was going to go all "rebel without a cause" with this guy. But having him make a responsible budget and put off gratification until he can afford it? That's crazy talk!

They went with national activities first, of course; it seemed Meg Atomic had smashed up Tempestuous pretty thoroughly last night, and Tidal was considering giving her a key to the city. "Huh," Aaron said aloud. "So that's where she was. Wonder what she was doing all the way over there?" He had a suspicion, but he didn't pursue it; if she wanted to go after some pharmaceutically-obsessed nitwit, that was her business.

Meg hadn't been the only superhero in the country working last night, of course; the announcer cycled on through the usual accounts of Mr. Ecosystem doing this and Radiological doing that, and a brief encounter with the Parliamentarian, a British superhero on temporary detachment to the States. There was a short blip about one of Meg's friends, Anna Domino, fighting the Time Looper in Vancouver. Aaron hadn't talked to Anna all that much, but she seemed nice enough.

Then another dramatic theme played, and the station's local news took over. Aaron picked up on the subtle differences in the theme, and his heart began to race. That wasn't the usual theme where they reported recent activities, no, this one meant breaking news. This meant-

"And it's confirmed, repeat, we have confirmed reports that Titanium Walrus has launched an attack upon the city zoo. Several superheroes are on the scene at this moment, but it seems Titanium Walrus brought reinforcements as well, and a full-scale battle has developed. We go live now to our correspondent Wendy

Day[14]; Wendy, can you give us more details on what's happening?"

Aaron didn't even bother listening to Wendy; he whipped his car around and started off towards the zoo as fast as he could go. Unfortunately he went right through a stop sign and got pulled over by a nearby police officer for a traffic violation, and by the time he'd showed his driver's license and his power permit and explained the situation, and the officer had checked with his superiors and run the permit through the system and delivered a stern warning to Aaron to be more careful next time, it was too late. The battle was over before he could get there.

It had been dramatic while it had lasted, though. Tasha hadn't even known Titanium Walrus had escaped from his confinement cell when she arrived in the zoo's parking lot a half hour before. She had unbuckled the Twins from their carseats and gotten them carefully outside, with stern admonitions not to run off and stay close by her side, which they immediately disregarded. Winston bobbed over to head them off, and at that moment the other moms saw them and waved. "Sorry I'm late," Tasha said when she joined the group, Jamie and Jeremy firmly in hand and Tamsin and Caden trailing behind. "The Twins today, you wouldn't *believe*..."

Audrey nodded sympathetically. *Philip has told me about his struggles with his own cloning ability when he was a child. I believe he still has some literature on the subject; I can lend it to you if you would like?*

---

[14] You can really tell the author put a great deal of thought into this character's name.

"Yeah, that'd be helpful," Tasha said, as Meredith floated over to where Caden was standing awkwardly a few feet off, scuffling at the ground.

Hello, Meredith 'pathed at him. *I was hoping you would come today.*

"Really?" Caden said.

Yes. Mother tells me the tram has reopened, and I was wondering if you wanted to ride with me. On the tram. It goes right past the elephants!

She pronounced that last word in the British way, almost as if she'd said "ellie-phants", and Caden's heart skipped. He loved the whole British accent. He wanted to say yes, but suppose he said something wrong? Spending so much time alone all night as he did, he didn't have the best social skills. He hesitated, flushing, his hands going sweaty. Tamsin giggled nearby. She was clearly about to burst into song again.

Fortunately for Caden, at that exact moment there was a sudden explosion from inside the zoo, and a heavily armored man smashed out through the front gate, flames belching from his rocket pack, and a small army of mind-controlled walruses staggering behind him. "Citizens of Edison City!" he boomed to the confused would-be zoo-goers in the parking lot. "I have come to liberate the walruses, and all marine mammals, from their captivity! Soon the world will tremble before the sound of our flippers!"

"Kids, stay back," Tasha said calmly, pushing Jamie and Jeremy behind her, as Winston dropped a protective ray shield around them. "You too, Tamsin, Caden. Get inside the shield. Mom's got to fight the supervillain now."

Caden, alarmed and yet oddly relieved, darted into the shield. Tamsin was more reluctant. "Can't I help? I can totally help! Please? Please please please please?" she whined.

"Tamsin Mariah Case, if you don't get inside that ray shield *right now...*"[15]

Tamsin, duly chastened, went inside the ray shield, not without making a rude face at her mother. Tasha would've corrected her for that, but she was in full Super Soccer Mom mode now. A panel on the Miraculous Minivan slid open, and five soccer balls floated out. These weren't nearly as technologically advanced as Winston; they only contained a hard core of explosives, and just enough circuitry for Super Soccer Mom to lock on to them with her brain and send them hurtling towards Titanium Walrus. Meanwhile, Audrey unleashed a shock wave of telekinetic power, and the other moms in the group let loose with their own abilities as well, and within seconds Titanium Walrus was down and whimpering, his armor suit pretty well shredded. The day had been saved once again.

This news was reported triumphantly by the Edison City media, with the result that Aaron turned his car around and headed back to work. He arrived just in time to be two seconds late. Fortunately his supervisor was an understanding sort and didn't fire him for his infraction; Aaron was so often on time anyway. And so he settled in to his usual routine of swiping widget bar codes with a scanner and sending them off to their destinations around

---

[15] Ooh, full name. With middle. That means she's serious. Good thing I'm not Tamsin.

the country, his mind wandering as he worked. He could now see sensibly that he wouldn't have been able to do much once he had got there; his power only worked in combination with other genuine superpowers, and Titanium Walrus wasn't technically super; he just had really good toys. In the end, he shouldn't have taken the risk at all. Power or no, Aaron had some time before come to the practical conclusion that he really didn't want to be a superhero exactly; he wanted to do his job and live his normal routine life. If occasionally he could help save someone, that would be fun, but he didn't live for it. And so he moved on from that, to working out the second verse of a praise chorus he was writing for the church youth group he played for on Saturday nights[16].

Little did he know[17] that the whole day's events had been closely observed by Candystriper, and a few other temporarily hired minions. Even Titanium Walrus had been part of the scheme, although he hadn't been told overmuch about his role, and none of it truthful. At any rate, the Malevolent Med-Student knew that a great deal of very useful intelligence had been gathered. True, Tamsin was probably no brattier than any normal child, but she could be pushed. The two oldest children still at home were clearly vulnerable, though in different ways. Sauna in particular...oh that was delicious. A ticking time bomb, and

---

[16] Hm. You know, maybe the author *should've* taken the rebel-without-a-cause approach with this kid. Right now he seems a bit, erm, how shall I put this delicately, boring. Boring like a boring thing that's...boring. Exactly.

[17] Now that's more like it. A dramatic lead-in! Sweet!

the parents didn't even know. How easily she could be pushed over the cliff. All that was needed was the push.

Chapter Three

Meg Atomic had almost, but not quite, been lured to sleep by the steady hum of the jet plane as it soared through the sky. She sometimes had trouble sleeping, especially when she'd been thinking through a perplexing problem, and she couldn't quite convince her brain to shut off and go to sleep. Even now, for example, her thoughts kept chasing themselves round and round like hyperactive gerbils in her head. The probability futures arranged themselves in neat patterns, and nearly every one distressed her immensely.

If the Malevolent Med-Student—no, *Drew*, she reminded herself, he'd asked her to use his real name—continued on as he had been, she very much suspected that he would be proposing to her. If he didn't, that meant he had put her squarely in the friend zone, a place she didn't want to be in at all. But if he did, that meant she would have a binary choice: yes or no. Yes meant she would have to explain to her parents that not only was she dating an ex-supervillain, but she had agreed to marry him. And she strongly suspected that her parents would dispute the *ex* part of ex-supervillain. The Malevolent Med-Student hadn't been in the minor leagues, after all; he'd pulled off some pretty major capers before he'd turned state's evidence against Queenpin. She would have to persuade them that he really had changed. This assumed that she had said yes, of course. Suppose she said no? *Could* she say no?

The chirp of her cell phone interrupted her musings. It wasn't entirely a distraction, though, since it was Drew himself who was actually calling. Meg ran through fifteen possible scenarios in the three seconds before she hit the talk button, ruling out a whole probability tree on the basis that he couldn't be so impolite as to propose via phone. "Drew?" she said.

"Margaret!" he said. "I hope your flight's going well? I wish I could've stayed to watch you take off, but you know how security is these days..."

"Yeah," Meg agreed, while mentally filing away the important data point that he was the only person she knew who routinely called her by her full name and that was—oh, *stop it*, she reprimanded herself. "I wish I had gotten Dad's flight powers. On the bright side, at least I do not set off the metal detectors every single time like Mom does."

They shared a laugh over that, though it wasn't all that funny, at least not to objective observers anyway, like a certain fictional character who keeps leaving annotated notes that interrupt the rhythm of the story[18]. Meg asked how he was doing, and Drew related the latest community service project he was helping with. Apparently he'd improved the efficiency of the Tidal chapter of the Red Cross by thirty percent, and completely reorganized their blood-donor filing system. This reminded him of something he'd read about a new line of genetic research that showed promise against a certain virus, and from there he and Meg had a tremendously complicated scientific conversation that would require two dictionaries and a doctorate to even get the gist of. Meg kept up her end of it wonderfully, though in the back of her mind she kept wondering what it all meant. This was the seventeenth long conversation she'd had with him. That had to mean their

---

[18] Hey now. Let's not get snippy. I happen to think my notes lend a certain air of verisimilitude. Besides, breaking the fourth wall, much?

relationship was progressing, didn't it? He was committing to her! This was quality time! And if that were the case, then a proposal really wasn't very far off.

She wondered if she should drop a subtle hint into the conversation, maybe something to let him know that she suspected where their relationship was going. Then he did something that completely threw her calculations for a loop. They had finished their discussion of complex genetic theory and were signing off. She said good-night as usual, and he replied, '"Night, Margaret. Love you," and then he disconnected before she could say anything.

The word. He had used *the word*. And not in a way like most guys used it, as in "Man, I love those Carbon Filaments. Great defense this year." No, he had said it exactly the way as a person serious in their relationship would've said it. He hadn't done that before. This was escalation! Meg's whole carefully plotted probability tree vanished in a puff of mental smoke. This required serious thought. She closed her eyes and went back over the exact phrase he had used, the tone in his voice, the correlation between that and the tone he'd used in the rest of the conversation, what she had said that might've sparked his startling sign-off, and on, and on, and on, as the plane flew on into the evening sky.

She might have had to redo her calculations again if she had overhead the call he had made next. The Malevolent Med-Student dialed another number on his cell phone. "Right," he said. "Start phase two. And make sure you-....is that a vuvuzela in the background? Why do you- oh. Candystriper. Of course. I am not even going to ask why she's playing a vuvuzela in the background. ....oh, Marcie told her to. She hasn't told you who Marcie is? Ah, well, Marcie is the tiny blue manatee that advises her on important ethical issues, like the shoulder angels you see in the cartoons, if those were manatees. Yes, it's stupid. Yes, she's a loony. But she's my minion, and come to think of it I'm not paying you to criticize my minion! Begin phase two! Quickly!"

He clicked his phone shut, muttering a few choice expletives. He really should've done this whole operation himself, but that just wasn't what one was supposed to do when one was putting a tremendously complicated Master Plan into action. Tradition meant that you hired others, lesser supervillains for the hero to fight through until they were ready to face you, in the climactic moments of the Master Plan. Of course, here, the Malevolent Med-Student's plan was even more subtle than that. He wished he could deliver a monologue about it; he had a lovely one prepared, but unfortunately Candystriper was away, and he didn't have any other minions around. Then he remembered that his phone had video capability, which meant he could deliver his monologue anyway and record it for Candystriper to listen to later. "Ah, technology," he exulted as he opened his phone again and hit *record*.

Back in Edison City, Aaron had just clocked out of his shift at Wally's Widget Factory. He walked out into the parking lot, enjoying the unseasonably cool late summer evening. His car was off near the far edge of the parking lot, just under a lamppost.

Marsha[19] was walking down the sidewalk near the parking lot, on her way home from her summer class at a university. She didn't pay any attention to Aaron as he casually strolled towards his car, for two very understandable reasons; neither of them knew each other, and she was already engaged in a conversation with a friend who was taking the same class with her. They were having a fierce debate about economics, which Aaron didn't much care for anyway, so he only made a polite nod as he passed them and unlocked his car door. At that precise moment a caped figure swooped down from the sky and smashed into the sidewalk so hard that his boots splintered the concrete[20]. He straightened to his full impressive height, and glared fiercely at the terrified women. For this was no poser, no mere ordinary villain like the Rogue Jaywalker. This wasn't even a powerless but still intimidating Titanium Walrus. No, this was a major villain, big leagues, multiple fights with the good guys, dramatic minor-key theme, everything. This was the Warthog.

"Hey," he rumbled, "ya know why you're like a banana and ice cream?"

"Um..." Marsha said.

"'Cause you're about to be split. In pieces. With my fist." He burst out in guttural laughter, while Marsha groaned in pain.

The trouble with the Warthog, despite his thoroughly intimidating exterior, was that he had read somewhere that villains were supposed to deliver killing

---

[19] Oh, way to bring back the Innocent Bystander from chapter one. I suspect something dramatic is about to go down.
[20] Told you.

puns before they commenced with the actual killing. Unfortunately the Warthog had a deplorable sense of humor, and an even more deplorable idea of what a good pun was. At this point both Marsha and her friend rather wished that he would just go ahead with the smashing and put them out of their misery.

The Warthog's laughter subsided, and he focused on what he was really there for. He drew back his powerful super-strong fist, and then hesitated, as he wasn't sure which of his victims he wanted to smash first. Then a new problem arose, as Aaron calmly stepped between him and his would-be prey. "I wouldn't do that if I were you," he said quietly.

"Ooh, tough guy!" the Warthog roared. "What're ya gonna do, huh? Punk?"

"I'm going to not let you smash these people, is what I'm going to do," Aaron rejoined. "And hey, my sister Sauna, she's real good with words, you should ask her for better lines."

The Warthog howled in outrage and lashed out towards Aaron, thoroughly intending to smash his head in; he could worry about the girls later. At least, he started to lash out towards Aaron. All of a sudden, though, his knees had gone oddly weak, and a wave of dizziness swept through him. His swing went awkwardly wide, and never even came close to Aaron. Then Aaron delivered his own punch, not a terribly effective one or even well-placed (he'd never quite learned the proper method of fist-fighting) but to the Warthog it felt as if he'd been run over by a rhino. He staggered and collapsed in an ungainly heap, overwhelmed with shock. "What...what did ya do..." he gasped.

Aaron sighed. "You wouldn't get it if I told you."

He turned around to make sure the girls were okay; they were, and both were very grateful for his help. Marsha was used to these sorts of things as she'd lived in Edison City all her life, but her friend had lived in a small rural town that didn't have so much as a slightly eccentric scientist, let alone supervillains or capes. She poured out her gratitude in a flood of incoherent words, and Aaron quite sensibly suggested that she should sit down, maybe have something to drink. By pure coincidence there happened to be a diner nearby, and she took up his offer very readily. "Jill," she introduced herself in tremulous tones, "and I've never, I don't even, he just flew out of the sky, and how did you? I never would've...what on..."

Aaron hadn't been in the mood to explain his power to the Warthog, but he decided that he really should explain to Jill, if only to alleviate her distress. "See, I don't have any superpowers on my own, but what I can do is turn other people's powers back on themselves. Reverse 'em, so to speak. So the Warthog's power is super-strength, so all of a sudden he's not so strong anymore. If he'd tried a freeze ray, which he doesn't have but I know a few guys that do, it might've bounced back and frozen him. You get the idea."

"That is *so cool!*" Jill said.

"Yeah," agreed Marsha. "Look, I gotta get home, I have homework to do. You gonna be okay to drive, or..."

Jill wavered. "I...I don't know..."

Aaron took his cue. "Maybe I could drop you off?" he offered politely.

"Yeah, that'd be good," she said. "Suppose he comes back?"

He didn't, but Aaron drove her home anyway. Along the way they exchanged cell phone numbers, and Jill promised to text later, once she had fully recovered herself. It was quite a shock to her system, coming in from the country and nearly getting pummeled by a mutant warthog before getting saved by someone with power-reversal abilities. Aaron said the usual things about how anyone would've done the same thing (which wasn't literally true as he was the only one he knew of who had that particular power, but Jill wasn't the sort to quibble about semantics). They parted on friendly terms, and Jill duly texted a few hours later. Aaron texted back, and they continued this exchange until fairly late that night. Jill naturally looked him up on Facebook and sent him a friend request, which he accepted with alacrity, and then they chatted on there for a while longer. Aaron wondered at the strangeness of it all. Jill, once she had calmed down, had proved to be a really interesting person. She was witty and funny, and knew some of the same songs he knew. Could this go somewhere?. If it did, he didn't think it'd be nearly as stressful at the Meg Situation his family was going through now, or at least he suspected they were going through. After all, it wasn't like Jill was a supervillain[21].

---

[21] That, dear readers, is what we in the novel business called foreshadowing. Of course, in other books it's done a lot more subtly; I think the author's being a bit too obvious here, but then maybe it'll all be fine. Maybe Jill is pure as the driven snow, and it's totally a coincidence that she met him right after the Malevolent Med-Student made that mysterious phone call. Right? Of course, right.

While Aaron was staying awake thinking about his love life, or lack thereof, Meg Atomic had landed from her flight and gone out on patrol. She found it a relaxing exercise, as she could focus entirely on the rhythm of fighting bad guys and let it distract her from the myriad problems worrying her. She calculated punches and strikes, worked out where the bad guy would be standing in the next several seconds and where she would want to be in order to trip him up, and generally applied physics in a beautiful symmetry of math and power. Meg rarely used her real super ability; making things explode at an atomic level was such an unstable power that she only deployed it for really serious emergencies.

Right now she had just dispatched a gang of jewel thieves who'd had the misfortune to rob a store on her patrol route. She landed a neat snap-kick into the midsection of the last remaining would-be burglar, folding him up like a rickety lawn chair. Some heroes in her situation, her father for example, would've delivered some sort of witty observation, or maybe a cautionary reminder to the burglar to mend his ways. Meg just left him whimpering on the sidewalk. He wouldn't have listened to her anyway.

She started to walk away when she heard a sudden thunderclap overhead. "Oh, bother," Meg exclaimed, knowing what that had to mean. If only she could turn invisible like her mom's friend Trina, or shapeshift into some inconspicuous object like her sister Tamsin (well, not quite like Tamsin, since a bright purple Frisbee isn't exactly the most inconspicuous thing ever). But she couldn't; all she could do was stand there and watch as Captain Happily

Married dropped out of the sky and landed in front of her. "Meg," he began, "I fear we need to have a discussion!"

"Dad, please, I am tired. I really just want to finish my patrol and go to bed. Could we just do this tomorrow?"

The captain sighed, and for once he dropped his monologue voice. "Meg, we really do need to talk. Maybe not tonight, but soon. We didn't know where you were the other night, and we had to adjust for that. We depended on your help, Meg."

"Yeah, well....I got a call in Tidal. Big emergency. Tempestuous attacked the harbor. I had to get there fast."

"But you could have at least called us to let us know," the captain pointed out reasonably. Then his eyes narrowed. "And what were you doing in Tidal anyway?"

Meg ran through a very rapid probability tree. She knew that he knew that the Malevolent Med-Student currently lived near Tidal. What she did not know was whether her mom had told him about her budding relationship with the ex-supervillain. She guessed not; otherwise he would've confronted her directly about it already. The captain wasn't one for subtle mind games. So that left her with two choices. She could come clean and tell him, but she could predict all sorts of reactions, and none of them were particularly pleasant. Or she could lie. The problem with that was that the captain would probably talk to her mom about it, and her mom would know that Meg had lied. Would her mom betray her confidence? Meg wasn't sure. Perhaps there was a third option. If she could smooth things over quickly, the captain wouldn't necessarily need to discuss it with her mom, he would move on to something else and forget about it. He was so linear that way.

"I was visiting a friend," she explained. "You know Anna lives out there[22]. I planned to be back well in time to watch the kids, but then Tempestuous attacked, and everything went pear-shaped. I am sorry."

Captain Happily Married felt, if not entirely mollified, at least a little relieved. Anna was trustworthy, he knew; he'd played golf with her father on Saturdays before they had moved out to their new base in Tidal. "Well, next time, if an emergency such as that does arise, you might at least try calling us. Even if just for a second. We were worried, you know. But on the bright side, I saw the reports about your victory over Tempestuous. A brilliant escapade!"

"Yeah, it was," she said, knowing she had averted the crisis when he went back into his monologue voice. "I am just glad no one was seriously injured. The Tidal EMTs could give lessons to the ones here."

"Indeed they could!" the captain said. "I still do not think it was a wise decision to let the Malevolent Med-Student off without incarceration, but if he must be out on the streets, at least he's using his abilities productively[23]."

"Drew certainly has helped them out. He reorganized the local Red Cross chapter, made them thirty percent more efficient, and..." she froze, suddenly realizing her mistake[24].

---

[22] Oh, that's clever. Both those things are true on their own; they're misleading when you put them together, since she's implying she was visiting with Anna, not Drew, which she actually was. But I don't think Captain Happily Married's going to pick up on that. This girl should go into politics.
[23] Uh-oh. Warning! Warning! Bail out, Meg! Run! Run!
[24] And...too late. She's in for it now.

Captain Happily Married frowned. "*Drew?* Since when are you on a first-name basis with the Malevolent Med-Student? And...come to think of it, I also remember seeing a report that Anna was in Vancouver on the day you were fighting Tempestuous, going after the Time Looper! She wouldn't have been in Tidal at all, which I'm pretty sure is what you said." Comprehension dawned, like a computer booting up and making the cheery welcome tone, although this comprehension wasn't nearly so cheery. "You weren't with her at all. You were with...the Malevolent Med-Student! You skipped out on your commitment to our family so you could date a supervillain?"

"*Ex*-supervillain," Meg shot back. "He promised to change his ways, and he is really doing it!"

"Do you know how often I have seen so-called *ex*-supervillains promise to change their ways, and then turn back to villainy the moment they get the chance?" the captain thundered. "He blew up a whole pharmacy only last year!"

Meg rolled her eyes in exasperation. "*Again* with the pharmacy! Mom brought up the same thing; I told her, it was an abandoned building, there were no civilians inside-"

Captain Happily Married blinked. "You...told her? But she said nothing about this to me. She just said that we'd talk about it later."

"Well, maybe she didn't trust you!" Meg said, casting calculation to the wind and not really thinking about what she was saying. "Maybe she thought you'd do something stupid like fly off to Tidal and attack him!"

She really should've learned not to say those sorts of things to the literal-minded captain. "An excellent idea!" he said, his mighty fists clenching in anger. "And when I return, Margaret, you and I and your mother are going to have a very serious conversation!" With that he rocketed off into the sky before Meg had a chance to say anything.

Her eyes flamed. Light shone starkly from her hands, snapping away her shadow. For one second, Meg seriously considered opening fire on the captain. She could swat him from the sky like an errant bug, she knew. Hadn't she done the same thing to Thunderdomestic only last year, and wasn't she at least as strong as the captain was? Didn't she have the power?

But then the fire in her eyes died and the harsh light in her hands went dim. Meg couldn't do that. Not to her own father, no matter how much he infuriated her. Because he was still her father, and she cared very much for him, and besides, they were both superheroes, and superheroes did not attack each other. The trouble was, she had no idea what to do now. Should she call Drew and warn him? Or would that make things even worse? The probability trees ran themselves out in her mind, but none of them ended in a happy place. Then she heard a clatter nearby; whirling, she saw that one of the burglars had apparently recovered and was trying to make a getaway. Meg's eyes flamed again. For this moment, she knew exactly what she could do.

In a nearby alleyway (they really were the most wonderful spots for surveillance), Candystriper sent a text message to her boss. It was mostly emoticons and text-speak, but the substance was that Captain Happily Married was on his way, and he was not happy. Candystriper strongly recommended that her dear Mal-Meddie take cover, and she emphasized her concern by adding no fewer than five exclamation points to the end of her sentence.

To her surprise, the Malevolent Med-Student texted back only a brief acknowledgment, without a single emoticon of concern. Had he not understood her? Granted, sometimes Candystriper didn't understand herself, but she had thought she was pretty clear. She texted again, an even more fervent reminder that he really really needed to get out of Tidal[25].

The Malevolent Med-Student sent back two sentences. *Don't panic. This is completely within my brilliant, villainous plan.* Candystriper wasn't exactly reassured. She had seen the Malevolent Med-Student's brilliant, villainous plans fall apart one too many times. But then she decided that maybe this time was different, and maybe he would win this one, and hey, an ant was crawling across her shoe. She bent down to observe the ant, forgetting about her leader's troubles entirely. As it turned out, she needn't have worried.

---

[25] Yeah, that's why you should listen to your minion, folks. If I ever became some sort of tyrannical mistress of all evil, like Maleficent or Susan or someone, I'd be sure to be very respectful towards my minions. You never know when one of them might have a decent idea.

Chapter Four

Captain Happily Married cracked through the western skies at nearly supersonic speeds. Deftly he dodged thundering jet planes, streaked uncaringly past startled flocks of geese, blazed right into storm systems and right out again. He was operating in pure battle-mode now. The Malevolent Med-Student had imperiled his daughter. He didn't know what had possessed her. Meg was a sensible person; she wouldn't do something like this. She would know not to date a supervillain, especially not the Malevolent Med-Student. Not unless he'd gotten to her somehow. He had access to a whole range of unhealthy pharmaceuticals; maybe he'd drugged her. That thought made the captain even more wrathful than before, and gave an extra edge to his speed.

Somewhere over Colorado he became aware that his utility-belt phone was ringing. He checked the readout, scowled, then slowed his flight down enough so that he could communicate without having the phone fly off into the stratosphere. "Tasha," he said flatly, before she could even say anything. "Did you know about this thing with the Malevolent Med-Student?"

Silence. A silence that went on entirely too long. Then, "Meg...did say something about him, yes."

"And you didn't tell me."

"I didn't think....I was hoping she would come to her senses on her own. I was hoping we wouldn't need to get involved."

"Well," Captain Happily Married said, coming closer to using improper language than he had ever been before in his life, "When a supervillain like him intends to date my daughter, I think we pretty well *should* get involved! Maybe if we had gotten involved before now, this wouldn't have happened!"

"Maybe not, but I don't see what we can do about it now. She's an adult, Justin. She can make her own decisions."

"Not this time she can't," the captain said.

Tasha breathed an exasperated sigh. "Dear, why don't you just come home and we'll talk about this, okay? I can call Meg, she'll be up anyway I'm sure, and we'll work all this out-"

"Sorry, Tasha, I don't think that's going to happen. I'll be in late tonight."

"And where exactly....you're *not* going where I think you're going."

For the first time that evening, Captain Happily Married smiled. "Let's just say Drew and I are going to have a friendly father-to-boyfriend...chat[26]." He disconnected before Tasha could respond, then powered back up to supersonic speeds. He was actually beginning to look forward to this, now.

"That *idiot*," Tasha said, slamming the phone down. Rarely had she ever been so angry with Justin. He could've taken the reasonable path, come back home, and had a civilized discussion about their dilemma, but no, he had to go and play the overprotective dad cliché. There was only one thing to do. "Winston," she said as she went for her uniform, "power up the minivan. Run a diagnostic on the

---

[26] Ooooh, bad Cap, bad Cap, watcha gonna do? Whatcha gonna do, when he comes for you?

fuel cells; we'll have to go supersonic if we're going to catch up to him, and we'll need plenty of power. Actually, no, strike that, he's got enough of a head start that we won't catch him just by flying. Radio Audrey, send my apologies if she's asleep, but tell her I really need her to 'port me out to Tidal, stat."

She pulled on her boots and tied on the blue-purple cape she wore; Tasha had heard that capes were going out of style, but she kept hers nonetheless. Sentimental reasons, probably. She walked quickly out into the hallway, still thinking aloud as Winston bobbed behind her. "Okay, he'll have flown the straight route out there, but he probably won't know exactly where he's going. Tidal is a big place. Winston, see if you can find out where the Malevolent Med-Student's located. An address, post office box, Facebook check-in, secret lair, anything. I'll probably beat him there if I can get specific coordinates and have Audrey 'port me right to them." She checked the time readout on one of Winston's panels. "Hope's probably asleep by now. I don't know who else I could get this late. It could be fine; Aaron's here, and I'll be back quick. I hope." She hadn't thought much about what she was going to do when she got there, other than the vague idea of stopping her husband from pounding the Malevolent Med-Student into a pulp. But then it occurred to her: exactly how was she going to do this? Reasonable persuasion? That hadn't exactly worked when she was communicating with him before. She did have her exploding soccer balls....but Tasha had never used her power against Justin before. There'd only been one time she'd used it against another hero, and that had been because the poor girl had been mind-controlled by Admiral Zombie Lady. She had never attacked a fellow hero in full possession of his or her own mind. And she had especially never attacked Justin.

Could she do it? Tasha honestly didn't know. She'd never thought about it. Then she wondered what that might do to him; he'd told her long ago that his powers weren't your garden-variety genetic enhancement or gamma-radiation type, no, his powers in some mystical way derived from his marriage. Thus his superhero name. If she used her own abilities against him, would that hurt their marriage somehow? She'd heard stories of other hero couples who had turned on each other, and after the laser blasts and the ray shields had died down, they had gotten divorced. Tasha had worked to keep that from happening, although it had been easier than she thought, given that her husband was who he was. Their marriage had been a little less rocky than the norm, and she'd been proud of that. Sure, they'd had spirited discussions on occasion, and even the odd quarrel, but they'd always made up afterwards, and then when the kids had started coming they had just been too busy to fight. Now she wondered; if she was forced to use her powers against him, could their marriage survive?

It had to, she decided. They could make up afterwards; they'd always had. He would understand, when he came to his senses. And she didn't have time to think about it anyway; Audrey's voice echoed in her mind. *I am outside, whenever you are ready.* She didn't sound tired, but Tasha assumed that was due to the nature of telepathy. She would have to apologize to her friend later. Right now she didn't have the time. She poked her head into Aaron's room and was about to wake up him when she realized he was already up and texting someone. Tasha vaguely wondered who; Aaron had never been much for the texting. But she couldn't think about that now. "Aaron," she whispered quickly. "I have to run out. Superhero emergency. You know the drill. Keep an eye on the others."

"Right," Aaron acknowledged. He had done the same thing before, on those rare occasions when there wasn't time enough to get a licensed sitter before Tasha and the Captain had to run off to save the world. He assumed this was another of those times. Tasha decided not to tell him the real nature of the emergency; he didn't need to know, and it would all be dealt with soon anyway. She dashed outside, Winston racing behind. "I won't be taking the minivan," she explained breathlessly to Audrey. "Just me and Winston. And, oh, almost forgot," she sent a thought towards the minivan, and three of her exploding soccer balls flew to her. "Thanks a bunch, Audrey, I owe you."

Do you need me to accompany you? Audrey 'pathed in concern. *I could help-"*

"No, 'preciate it, but this thing's personal," Tasha said, which was entirely true. Just how personal was something Audrey didn't need to know either. "Winston should have the coordinates for you." The soccer ball projected a green laser hologram of the coordinates in the air.

Audrey shrugged, and raised her hand. Light flashed around Tasha, and within seconds Tidal resolved itself into clarity around her. It was still late evening there, as the sun hadn't entirely gone down yet, still hovering just above the horizon of the western sea. She checked to make sure Winston and her exploding soccer balls were with her, and took off running down the sidewalk. Apparently

Winston had directed her to the Malevolent Med-Student's apartment, just down the street. It looked like she'd beaten her husband there; maybe he wouldn't even show up at all. Maybe she wouldn't have to-

Then she heard a distinctive thunderclap overhead, and sighed wearily. It looked like she would have to do this after all.

Meanwhile, back at her house, Audrey had teleported away again, puzzled by the night's events but assuming that Tasha knew what she was doing. Aaron, meanwhile, made a cursory check of the house; it looked like everything was shipshape. The Twins were fast asleep in their bunkbeds, Caden was calmly playing a video game, and Tamsin was lying sprawled out on her bed, her feet where the pillow normally was, having evidently decided to try the novel experiment of sleeping the other way round. She seemed comfortable enough, and Aaron decided not to bother her. He'd never understood his sisters. Sauna's door was closed as always; Aaron didn't hear anything inside, so he assumed she'd gone to sleep as well. Couldn't tell with her, really, with her going all weird and emo and all. He decided to stay awake a little longer, as he hadn't quite finished chatting with Jill.

What Aaron didn't know was that Sauna wasn't asleep. She had heard Tasha whispering to Aaron, and wondered what was going on. She caught the tail end of her mother's instructions, then heard her running down the steps and out the door. Sauna ran to her window, in time to see her mother and Winston disappearing in a flash, evidently teleported somewhere. Sauna's hands tightened on the sill. This was *so* not fair. She was 15, for heaven's sake, practically old enough to get a power permit; she did *not* need looking after, especially not by her brother who was only a bit older than she was. Plus, she had just been meaning to talk to her mom, having almost worked up the nerve to confess her recent problems, or at least hint at them anyway. She didn't know if her mom had ever had issues like that, but maybe she knew someone who had. But she couldn't ask her now, could she? Nooooo. It was so unfair! So totally...not...*fair*.

Steam blossomed around her, and red light spilled between her fingers. Sauna felt a shock of terror as she realized what was happening. She grabbed for her ukulele but it was clear across her room, and before she could go for it she realized it was already too late. Sauna made a start towards the door of her room, and realized she couldn't; there were too many flammable things in the rest of the house, not to mention flammable people. She had to get out of there *now*, before the red light blazing from her went white and devoured everything she knew in fire. There was only one way left. Sauna ran to her window, the glass warping and shattering at her touch. She plunged outside without even thinking, blazing out of her window like a falling star. She hit the ground hard, and pain lanced through her, but Sauna staggered upright without caring, desperate to get as far away from her house as she could. Grass burst into flame under her feet as she limped forward. Then she heard an alarm shrieking loudly. In her distress and terror, she couldn't help thinking that it sounded oddly familiar. Not quite like a normal fire alarm, almost like...she realized what it was about two seconds before it didn't matter anymore.

The Miraculous Minivan was truly a wonderful machine. Not only did it have jet thrusters and car-seat stabilizers, it also had fully capable fire-suppression systems. Unfortunately for Sauna, the Miraculous Minivan's fire systems weren't about just foam. Super Soccer Mom had gotten in contact with a friend of hers from Denmark who had studied cryogenics. White energy beams shot from the minivan, lasering in unerringly on the unusual heat source the minivan's computers had detected. In seconds Sauna was encased entirely in block of ice, her heat extinguished, frozen solid in suspended animation. Jill emerged casually from the shadows, a shovel in her hand. "You need to learn to chill," she said, and giggled. It wasn't the wittiest of puns, but it was the best she could do, given that she hadn't prepared anything and had to improvise.

Then she glanced down at the shovel, and her eyes glowed. Two purple beams shot from them and zapped the shovel, whereupon it floated away from her hand and hovered above the door. Jill hadn't been entirely forthcoming with Aaron about her civilian status; she had powers, alright. She could magnetize and control anything she zapped with her Magneta-Beams, so long as she had the thing within line of sight. It wasn't as impressive as, say, being able to manipulate fundamental electromagnetic forces, but it was useful in its way. For example, when Aaron came hurrying out the door, having heard the commotion outside, she merely blinked, and the shovel flashed down and whacked him on the back of the head. He never should've told her that he didn't have powers of his own. That made him vulnerable. And that was all she needed.

Jill stepped over his unconscious form and went inside to finish up. She didn't quite understand her orders, but they'd been clear enough, and her boss didn't like being questioned. Besides, she was on a tight schedule. Candystriper would be coming soon. And Candystriper, well....she was crazy enough that she would stick to her orders like Holy Writ, especially if they didn't make sense. Jill didn't want to be around when Candystriper showed.

An hour or so later, Candystriper duly arrived, lugging a device that looked like an oversized telescope, except with a few too many sharp pointy bits, and a very big red button that should've indicated to any normal person that it should under no circumstances be pushed. Candystriper, being anything but normal, took aim at the house and pushed it.

A short pause followed, and she wondered if her dear Mal-Meddie's brilliant plan had fallen through again. She was about to pack it up and go home when the house exploded in a single intensely white flash, like a second sun. The shockwave blew out windows for blocks in every direction, and sent Candystriper headlong into the sky like a stray leaf caught in a tornado Even as she hurtled head over heels through the air, Candystriper had time for one questioning thought. Maybe, just maybe, she should've listened when Marcie told her not to borrow the Kaboominator.

Meg had finished up the last of the jewelry store robbers, and was walking back to her apartment, trying to convince herself that maybe things would work out. Maybe her father would realize that Drew really had changed.

Maybe they would sit down together and have a civilized conversation in which Drew would be honest about his intentions and the captain would realize that his daughter really was an adult now, and a sentimental Hallmark moment would develop, and they would all live happily ever after. "Right. And maybe I will find a Shetland pony waiting for me on my doorstep," Meg said sarcastically to no one in particular.

  Then the flash came, lighting up the night sky like day. Windows shattered around her, and trees bent beneath the blast as if they were caught in a hurricane. Meg started running almost automatically; she knew explosives better than anyone in the city, and she knew whatever bad guy had deployed that needed to be stopped right then before he did it to anyone else. She had a motorcycle parked nearby; she swung aboard and raced off down the street, aiming for the general direction of the blast. She heard sirens wailing already, and knew the Edison City paramedics would be rushing to the scene. If that blast had been as powerful as she thought, Meg could only imagine the injuries and devastation. She might not be able to go after the supervillain if she was needed to help with the rescue efforts, of course there would be other superheroes helping too, and her brain began to run through a probability tree of the benefits of her help against the possibility that she could stop whatever it was from being used again, and...suddenly it dawned on Meg that the route she was taking towards the place where the flash had come from seemed awfully familiar. She knew these streets, didn't she? She had driven down them for years. This was where....and she gunned her motorcycle harder, her hands tightening in white-knuckled desperation on the handles.

Her heart raced in fear, her mind already going to the unthinkable. She frantically assured herself that she was worrying over nothing, that her family would be alright, her mom would've gotten everyone out in time and maybe the blast hadn't even been *near*....

Meg rounded the corner onto the street where her family had lived, and skidded to a stop. Her mouth fell open in horror. Where her house had once been, nothing remained except a single crater, gaping like an open wound. Fires ringed the hole, blazing in the wrecks of cars or shattered trees. The Miraculous Minivan lay crumpled up on its side like a child's toy thrown away, twisted and wrenched, its sides bashed in as though it had been beaten by a giant sledgehammer. Water sprayed into the air from torn-open pipes and a fire hydrant that had been ripped clean from its place.

She staggered off her motorcycle and took a few faltering steps forward, dimly aware that paramedics and firefighters were coming onscene. "Mom?" Meg said in a gasping breath. "Caden. Tamsin. Sauna. Aaron. Jamie. Jeremy, *Mom!*" She tripped and fell against the buckled roadway, then scrambled upright again and ran for the edge of the crater. No one answered her pleas. All that was inside the crater was dirt and fire. Meg collapsed to her knees, her face white with shock and pain. She hadn't seen this coming. All her probability trees, her intelligence, her incredible powers, and she hadn't seen this coming at all. She didn't even know who might have done it.

But that thought caused her eyes to turn as yellow as the fires still crackling around the crater. Whoever had done this thing would pay. Oh, would they pay. Meg would see to that. Her mind raced through cold calculations of which of Edison City's villains could have pulled this off, even as she came automatically to her feet and began the weary trek back to her motorcycle, brushing off the paramedics who offered help. She dismissed the Rogue Jaywalker out of hand. The Warthog didn't have the brains. Decedent Man had the resources with all the estate tax fraud he had pulled off, but she couldn't see a motive. Admiral Zombie Lady was in jail, and explosives weren't her style anyway. Titanium Walrus....there was a possibility. True, he'd been captured, but maybe he had escaped, or he'd had a backup plan. Meg was going to find out, one way or the other. She reached her motorcycle and was about to climb on when she paused, struck by a sudden terrible thought. What was she could to say to her father? The captain would have to be told. And she was going to have to tell him; she couldn't let him hear it from the news. She couldn't bear to have some impersonal reporter like Wendy Day be the one to break it to the captain that he had lost his wife and nearly all his family....and Meg broke down then, her cries ripping out of her like a wounded animal. But even as tears blinded her eyes and streaked down her face, she still managed to grab for her communicator. Somehow she had to tell him. The captain needed to know[27].

The captain was, at that moment, thundering in over the skies of Tidal. He hadn't thought about how

---

[27] Wow, this story sure took a turn for the serious. Don't worry, though, I'm sure all Captain Happily Married's kids are alive and well. I mean, the author wouldn't dream of nearly wiping out the poor guy's family, right? ....*Right?*

exactly he was going to locate the Malevolent Med-Student until only a few moments before as he'd blazed over the Rockies; fortunately, a solution had easily presented itself. Captain Happily Married blasted straight into downtown, slamming in for a hard landing on the elegant marble steps outside the federal courthouse building. He charged inside and went right through the metal detectors, sending the security guards into a flurry of activity that didn't do much of anything useful, since the captain had already gone up to the second floor and stormed into the small office of Walter Flowers, the Tidal district attorney. "Hey, Cap, what's-"

"The Malevolent Med-Student. Where is he."

Walter blinked. "Why do you need to know?" he asked cautiously.

"He's doing it again, Walter," the captain said, his voice oddly wavering. "The same thing he did with Elm Spirit. And this time he's with *my daughter.*"

"Oh..." Walter said bleakly, and sat down. "Blast."

They looked at each other's eyes, both remembering the same thing. The Malevolent Med-Student, with the capable if not entirely comprehending assistance of his loyal minion Candystriper, had blown up an abandoned pharmacy as a diversion for his real scheme; he and Queenpin had attempted to steal a vial containing an extremely lethal virus. Intelligence suggested he had meant to sell it to the Suzistanis, after refining it into an even more lethal virus that made the first one look like the common cold, thus the government had gotten involved. Worse yet, in his civilian identity he had befriended Elm Spirit, one of the superheroines stationed in Tidal, and then during a casual date he had laced her soft drink with enough pharmaceuticals to give even the strongest-willed superhero hallucinations for a week. He'd then convinced Elm Spirit that the military base out in Amethyst Bay was actually the site for an invasion of aliens determined to messily devour all the world's trees, and in her wacked-out state she believed every word. Captain Happily Married had fought alongside her father once; she was practically like another daughter. But because he knew her better than any of the other heroes, he had been called in, and forced to stop her. It hadn't been pretty. She was still going through recovery.

The captain had captured the Malevolent Med-Student in the end, but then to his dismay the government had come in and offered a deal. The Malevolent Med-Student had flipped on Queenpin and his Suzistani contacts to boot; in return he had been allowed to walk. The captain had managed to prevail upon the district attorney to at least impose a condition that prohibited the Malevolent Med-Student from making contact with his minion Candystriper, and especially with any other superheroines such as Elm Spirit. Unfortunately, because of the connection with the Suzistanis and the extremely sensitive nature of intelligence operations, most of the events had been classified top-secret. No one knew what the Malevolent Med-Student had done to Elm Spirit, or that he had nearly loosed a deadly virus on the world. He had just quietly been dropped from the news coverage, and meantime Drew Smith had set up his normal life in Tidal. Only a few people in the caped community even knew who Drew had been, and they had heard only that he had reformed, gone clean. Meg had known a bit about Queenpin, but she didn't know all of it.

The captain hadn't even told Tasha all of it. He hadn't told her of the fear that had crept inside him every night that something could happen to Meg Atomic. He hadn't told her of the heartbreak he had felt when he had been forced to knock Elm Spirit through a wall to keep her from smashing a military policeman who in her wild imaginings she saw as an alien invader. He hadn't explained the guilt he'd felt ever since, or the grim determination never to let that happen again. And now...now it was happening again.

"Right," Walter said, making a snap decision. "You'd better bring him in. I've honestly been thinking about going after him anyway; we've had unconfirmed reports that he's made contact with Candystriper, and at least one other individual. We don't know what he's up to, but it's obviously something big. I've got the coordinates of his apartment; it's on Malcolm Street, near the bay. The Taylor Building, number 5-F. " He pulled up a map on his computer and swung the display so Captain Happily Married could see.

"Right," the captain said. "I have them. You'll be seeing us shortly."

"Good luck," Walter said somberly. "You shouldn't have too much of a problem fighting him; our intelligence suggests he never did get the Kaboominator, and we haven't gotten word of any other armaments. He might have enhanced reflexes, who knows what he's been taking, but you should still be more than a match for him."

The captain saluted, and blasted out again, flashing right by the security guards who were just coming up to arrest him. Walter ordered them to stand down and apologized to the irate guard captain whose metal detector had been bent all out of kilter in the wake of the captain's passing. Sometimes, Walter reflected, he very much wished he didn't live in a world with superheroes. It would make his job so much less stressful.

Chapter Five

Captain Happily Married's communicator chirped in his utility belt, but he paid no attention; whoever it was could call back later. He had work to do. He blasted across the city skies and came in hard, crashing into the sidewalk in front of the Malevolent Med-Student's apartment building. He was about to flash in and track down the supervillain when he saw a familiar face in his peripheral vision. The captain whirled, completely taken aback. "*Tasha?*"

"Justin," she said calmly, a bit too calmly, "We need to talk."

"About what?" the captain said, a little obviously.

"You know. I can't let you go after Meg's boyfriend like this. You're wildly overreacting."

Images of Elm Spirit's contorted face flashed through the captain's mind. "Tasha, you have no idea what's going on. You don't know what he's done."

"I know what Meg has told me, which is that he's helped out the Tidal Red Cross and several other charities, and that he really has tried to reform. I don't know if I trust him entirely, but Meg seems to, and at the very least we have to let her make that call herself. She'd never talk to you again if you did what you're about to do, you know that."

The captain wanted to explain, but so much of the explanation was classified. "Tasha, please, just trust me on this. I'll explain what I can later, but right now-"

But Tasha had moved to the apartment steps, blocking his way, her face grim, as three soccer balls floated in behind her. "Justin, I'm sorry. But I can't let you. We're superheroes, we have too much power to abuse it like this."

She was thinking of a flashback too, something she hadn't told him either. She'd had a cousin, Lepton Lass, who'd been her closest friend when she was growing up, as she'd been an only child and an introvert. They had done everything together, even double-dated at prom. Or at least they'd tried to; Tasha's boyfriend (this was before the captain) had shown up on time, but Lepton Lass's hadn't. It turned out he had dumped her for someone else. Lepton Lass had taken things into her own hands, unleashing her incredible sub-atomic powers to the fullest. Tasha had never quite gotten those visuals out of her mind, especially the crater that had been the boyfriend's car. Last she heard he had made a full recovery and done okay for himself, but Lepton Lass had been captured and sent away. Tasha had never seen her again. She'd told herself many times over the years that no one blamed her; to be honest they had been growing apart anyway before that night. On the other hand, Tasha couldn't escape the thought that she should've noticed, should've seen that her cousin was becoming unstable. Now she was convinced that her husband was going down the same path, and she had to head him off before he went the way of her cousin.

"You do not understand!" Captain Happily Married exclaimed, slipping into his monologue voice. "He's a supervillain, he's already made contact with Candy-"

But at that moment Winston raced it, shrilling the highest-pitched alarm either of them had ever heard. "Winston, what-" Tasha started to say, then her eyes went wide in shock. "The house. It's been attacked. Oh my-"

"Tasha. The kids. Who did you leave them with."

"I didn't," she replied in a stunned voice. "I told Aaron. I thought..."

"Aaron only has a permit, he's not fully licensed yet!"

"*I know!*" she screamed. "I didn't think anything would happen, I thought I'd just talk to you and you'd come to your senses, and we'd be back before something happened!"

"Something *always* happens, Tasha," Captain Happily Married said, his eyes blazing. "You should know that. That's why we always leave a fully-licensed superhero with them, because something *always* happens!"

Before Tasha could snap back, light blossomed on the sidewalk between them, resolving itself into Meg's tear and dirt-streaked form. She glanced around, saw her mother, and ran to her. "Mom, thank heaven, I thought I'd lost you too, I..." she broke down in incoherent sobs.

Tasha hadn't had to comfort Meg like this since she'd been a small girl crying over the death of a character she'd seen in a movie. "It's okay, Meg, I'm here, I'm fine, I..." then she realized the full import of her daughter's words. "What do you mean, you thought you'd lost me *too?*"

"Meg," the captain said, "where are the kids?"

Meg couldn't say anything. She didn't have to. Winston was still shrilling in the background, but his readouts only conveyed what was already dawning on them. The captain wavered on his feet, as if he'd taken a mortal blow.

Tasha's mouth worked, but she couldn't say anything for a long moment. Then, suddenly, something snapped inside her brain. Just like that, without any warning. "Justin...it's your fault," she said, very calm, very quiet. "I would've been there if it hadn't been for you. I should've been there. I would've been. But no. I was here. Because of you."

"Tasha, I..."

She held up her hand. "No. No, I can't...I can't do this. I'm sorry. But it's your fault. And I can't...I can't stay with you when I'll have to think of this every day, every minute. So, I can't stay. I can't." Winston drifted sadly to her, piping mournfully. "Flight mode," she said, her voice steady. Two small jets emerged from Winston's side, and a zip-line attachment dropped down, which Tasha held onto. The soccer ball lifted off, carrying her into the sky. But before she disappeared into the night, Meg saw a thin golden circlet fall from her hand. It spun once against the sidewalk, and then fell flat.

There was a flash of red and white, and a sudden clap of thunder shook the city street. Captain Happily Married...changed. His uniform shirt went from red to solid black. His cape turned grey. His powerful form seemed to streamline, his superpowered muscles becoming more taut, more...dangerous. Meg knew at once what must have happened, though she had never seen her father before he'd become the captain. Without his marriage, his mystical powers had gone. But what was left? "Dad?" she said falteringly.

The former captain closed his eyes, and said nothing for a long moment. When he finally spoke, his voice was colder, harder, and definitely a whole lot more gravelly, like the kind of voice one gets when one has a really bad cold. "Yeah."

"Are you..."

"Okay? No. Capable? Yeah. My old persona didn't have all the captain's abilities, but the corporal had enough."

Meg gasped. "The Corporal? You mean you were..."

"Yeah. Corporal Abstinence."

She had known he hadn't been the captain before he had got married, but she had never learned his other identity. Corporal Abstinence was a name whispered in terror in the underworld of Edison City. Some still remembered the flashing of the throwing metal As in the moonlight, the swift lightning strikes and sudden raids, the complete demoralization as criminal rings were ferreted out and dismantled. He'd even gone after corrupt politicians a time or two. Captain Happily Married had been like sunlight after a storm. Now Meg felt the storm coming again, and she didn't much like it at all.

She was about to say something, though she had no idea what, when she suddenly realized where she was. She had been in such a hurry to get there, especially when she'd contacted Audrey and learned that her mom was still alive, that she hadn't asked for coordinates before the teleporting. Now she saw. Meg had already lost so much that night; she could not bear to lose anyone else she cared about, and she really did care about Drew. "Dad," she began hesitantly, "what...what are you going to do now?"

Corporal Abstinence shot a glance from her to the apartment building, and his eyes narrowed. "I came here to have a chat with your boyfriend. I see no reason to change that."

"Really. No reason. Not after what just happened. Not after Edison City."

"Why would I need to go back to the city? Is there anyone left I could save? Besides, Tasha..." and for one second his new resolve almost slipped... "She's certain to go back anyway. It's inefficient for two superheroes to investigate the same thing; she'll have Winston, too."

"Dad," Meg said, "I do not want to fight you over this, any more than Mom did."

"Good."

"But," she went on, "I will. I am not going to let you attack my boyfriend." She moved to stand in between him and the apartment building, and her eyes flamed. "And you know I can stop you. Especially now."

"You're right," the corporal said. "You do have the power." He turned, and started to walk away.

The fire died in Meg's eyes, and she reached out towards him. "Look, Dad, I-"

In a blur of speed the corporal whipped around and snap-kicked Meg so hard she went unconscious before she realized she had been hit. "You have the power," he repeated. "But you don't have the skill."

Corporal Abstinence stepped over her fallen form and marched up the steps of the apartment building, his own eyes lit with fury. He was going to have a chat with the Malevolent Med-Student, oh indeed he was. Exactly the same sort of chat he had just concluded with his wayward daughter.

Meanwhile, back in her own timeline, Catrina slammed the book shut in a burst of wrath. "Those *idiots!*" she exclaimed. "Can't they see sense? Honestly!"

She had forgotten she was in a quiet coffee shop, and several of the patrons shot irate looks in her direction.

Catrina was in no mood to be deterred. She had been growing more and more upset as she had been reading, to the point that she hadn't even been leaving nearly as many comments as she had before. She was pretty sure that the author hadn't wiped out Captain Happily Married's whole family except for Meg, but she had been very much affected by the characters' distress over it. And worse, it was plain as anything to her that the Malevolent Med-Student was behind the whole thing. He had so obviously set them up, and manipulated them into going after each other by invoking the whole "overprotective dad" cliché. And now there the corporal was, walking right into a painfully obvious trap, and she couldn't see any way he could get out of it. Honestly, she just wanted to go in there and beat some sense into those people.

Then Catrina smiled, the slow half-smile that usually meant very bad things to people she didn't care for. Maybe this was her story after all. After all, she was the heroine. Stopping bad guys, or in this case saving the good guys from their own stupidity, was what she did. So why *shouldn't* she intervene?

A tiny golden light spilled over her shoulder, and a little angel materialized out of the air. "Catrina!" her shoulder angel piped in alarm. "Verily, you cannot do what I think you're about to do!"

"Can too!" Catrina retorted eloquently.

A puff of smoke appeared over her other shoulder, taking the form of her shoulder angel's diabolical counterpart. "Sure ya can!" her shoulder devil assured her. "Cause you're awesome! And you're way better developed than any of those two-dimensional walking clichés!"

"Ooh, ooh, pride!" her shoulder angel exclaimed, bouncing around in excitement. "Seven deadly sins material right there! You're not better than those characters are, you know that, and you've got no right to meddle!"

"Why not?" Catrina demanded. "They need my help! Isn't that plain?"

"But they've got to work this out for themselves!" the angel protested. "That's the point! They're supposed to learn, and grow, and mature as characters! They can't do that if you jump in and short-circuit the process! Just *think* about it, Catrina!"

Catrina had to admit this seemed reasonable. After all, she had learned a little from her *Catrina in Space* adventure, and one thing she had learned was to maybe think about things before she jumped off into them. So she paused and gave the matter some serious thought. This lasted exactly two seconds. "Okay, I thought about it. I'm going in!"

The angel then made a very serious tactical error. She might have persuaded Catrina to change her mind had she deployed other arguments, like, for example, flipping to the back of the book to see if the story worked out after all. But instead she chose to engage Catrina on the girl's own terms. "And just how exactly are you going to do that?"

Catrina hadn't quite considered this. How *was* she going to get inside the book? After all, it wasn't like she could just zap herself away and materialize inside, just like the tiny angel had materialized on her shoulder....then she smiled again. "I was hoping you'd ask, small angelic version of me. Because I think you can really help with that."

The angel looked aghast. "Why on earth would I help? I don't want you to go in there at all!"

"Well, it's either you or my little evil friend over here, and she'd probably do something like make me eat a kitten or sell my soul before she agreed, and I'd rather keep my soul, thanks. I'm very fond of it."

"She's got a point," the shoulder-devil agreed. "Though not with the kitten thing. That's just wrong."

The shoulder-angel sighed. "Fine. I'll get you in. But I want to go on record as stating I'm still completely opposed to this whole idea. It's going to wreck a perfectly good plot. You'll see."

"Your objection is duly noted," Catrina said, and ignited her Sporksaber, its red blade arcing out in a flare of energy and terrifying the coffee shop patrons to no end. "Let's get going, shall we?"

The angel waved its hands. Catrina vanished in a flash of golden light. The book that had been in her hand fell to the floor. The coffee shop barista, who had just been about to call the police on this crazy person that had shown up and started waving around strange weapons, took her hand from the phone and sighed in relief. The patrons settled about their business again, and everything went back to normal. For the moment, anyway.

At first, all Catrina saw was bright golden swirling light. Then slowly the light dimmed, resolving itself into recognizable structures. Catrina was still new to the modern world, and Edison City in particular, so at first she didn't quite recognize where she was. The book had been distressingly light on description too; there hadn't been street names or geographic features or anything. Sometimes a little florid prose could be useful, she reflected. In any event, she appeared to be standing on an ordinary suburban street, cookie-cutter houses extending in every direction. It was night-time, and the moon was out in full bloom, although you couldn't see very many stars what with the light pollution from the city. She glanced quickly around, but all of the houses appeared to be standing; not a single one had been unceremoniously replaced by a crater. "Well, at least she got me in," Catrina said. "Question is, where did she get me in *to?*"

"I'm not telling," the shoulder angel said snippily, tiny arms folded across her chest. "You're on your own from here."

Catrina shrugged. "Story of my life." Then she noticed that there seemed to be an awful lot of sirens going off. She didn't know enough to pick out yet which ones were police cars and which ones were ambulances or fire engines, but she could tell there were a lot of them, and they weren't all that far away. Catrina remembered what she had read about the destruction of the superheroes' house with the Kaboominator, and she flourished her blade. Those sirens had to be heading towards the crater. And from what she had read, so would Tasha. "I'll start with her!" she declaimed, and set off towards the sound of the sirens.

What neither she nor the shoulder angel had apparently noticed was that Catrina's shoulder devil wasn't with them anymore. Had they considered the question, they might have assumed that the shoulder devil simply hadn't gone with them into the story, that it had merely gone back to the Bad Place. They were wrong.

Across the country in Tidal, the Malevolent Med-Student was watching Corporal Abstinence move stealthily up the stairs towards his floor. Drew had hacked into the apartment building's security system and routed the video feeds to his laptop, precisely for this sort of situation. He wasn't terribly worried. This was all part of his brilliant plan. He had successfully convinced Meg Atomic to date him on a day when he knew she had been asked to babysit her kids. He'd known this would affect her parents and probably push them over the edge; the destruction of their home at just the right moment made the probability into a sure thing. Now Captain Happily Married didn't have his incredible strength anymore; true, his Corporal Abstinence persona was a formidable opponent, but it just wasn't the same. The Malevolent Med-Student had studied martial arts himself; he was pretty sure he could fend off the corporal's attacks. Then all he had to do was deal with Tasha, convince a devastated Meg to marry him, conveniently dispose of her after the wedding, and then her inheritance, which meant her entire family's property, would legally be his. That would include Winston the soccer ball, not to mention all of the captain's files, including his encrypted access codes to all sorts of superhero bases. It was a brilliant scheme, the most brilliant Drew had ever had, if he did say so himself.

"Brilliant my foot," piped a tiny voice. Drew jerked in surprise. There before him floating on a puff of black smoke, was a miniscule girl in a red shirt, waving a tiny pitchfork, with two horns poking from her dark hair. Drew blinked very slowly. She was still there. "Oh crap," he said, "I'm going crazy. Just like Candystriper. I was afraid of this."

"No, you're not crazy," the shoulder devil said. "You're just stupid. First off, you're giving yourself way too much credit. I mean, how could you possibly have predicted that both Tasha and the captain would come after you? Suppose they hadn't? Suppose Tasha had stayed home, which she might easily have done? Then you'd be facing Captain Happily Married right now, and that wouldn't end well at all. Or suppose Meg had gone home to talk with her mom about it? Then she'd be dead, wouldn't she, and your whole "marry her and kill her later" plan goes up in smoke. Incidentally, I've gotta know, did you really kill off all the other kids? Or did you just make it look like you did?"

"I'm not telling you!" the Malevolent Med-Student retorted. "You're likely just a figment of my imagination!"

The shoulder devil smirked. "I'll bet you didn't. You idiots never do. You never learn to kill off the good guys when you have the chance; no, you hold on to them just in case they might prove useful, or to prove some stupid point about your evilness, or because you're going to set up some elaborate death trap."

"I'll have you know I *did* kill them. Every last one. All vaporized by the Kaboominator."

"If you say so," said the shoulder devil, hardly convinced. "Only the author knows for sure. But then considering this story's all shot to pieces anyway now that Catrina's come in and wrecked it, well, who knows?"

Drew was more confused than ever. "What?"

"Forget it. You wouldn't understand. Look, here's the deal. I peeked ahead at the book, so I know what's supposed to go down. Corporal Abstinence is going to fight you. You're going to win. But you're not going to kill him, no, you're going to set up an elaborate death trap that includes him and Tasha both, and the other kids assuming you didn't get rid of them already, and Meg. You'll do your villain monologue like you always do, and somewhere in the middle you'll say something that'll make Tasha realize she really does love Justin, and he'll realize he really loves her, and they'll decide they want to stay married after all."

"That's not what's going to-" the Malevolent Med-Student started to protest. In truth it actually was, short of the part where Tasha realized she loved Justin; Drew had already started building the deathtrap in his secret lair, the Pacific volcano fortress known as Blackacre, because a supervillain lair just isn't right if it's not inside a volcano.

The shoulder devil barreled on. "This, of course, is when Justin turns back into Captain Happily Married. With one flex of his mighty matrimonially-powered muscles he'll smash free of your trap, release all his kids and Tasha, and then everyone will have a big dramatic fight and you'll end up dangling from a cliff, and he'll offer to save you, but you'll be so consumed by your hate and evilness that you'll plummet to your death rather than accept his help, and so they'll all live happily ever after. Except for you, of course. You'll be dead. And no, you won't be mostly dead, you'll be all the way dead, and no one is going to go through your pockets and look for loose change, because you'll have spent all your money on your stupid death trap."

Drew had to admit that the shoulder devil had a point. It was entirely possible that if he put Tasha and Justin in the same death trap together, that they would rekindle their relationship, and then things would go all pear-shaped. "Well....you have any better ideas?"

A slow smile spread itself across the shoulder devil's tiny face. "Now that you mention it..."

Corporal Abstinence had been slowly working his way up the stairs, dodging one elderly grandmother along the way with such stealth and skill that she didn't even notice his passing. He finally reached the fifth floor, slipped out into the hall, and located the Malevolent Med-Student's door. 5-F, there it was.

His eyes narrowed, focusing with utter precision. It had been a long time since he'd gone into his hand-to-hand combat mode; when one has boundless strength and speed, one doesn't really need to worry about precision. Fortunately, he found that it was like riding the proverbial bike. He tuned out everything he didn't need to know, like the janitor down the hall, or the ding of the elevator as it reached its destination. He zeroed in like a laser on the apartment door. One swift kick in a strategic spot and it would fly open. Then he would burst in, deploying his cape to maximum terrifying effect. After that he would simply snap-kick the Malevolent Med-Student into unconsciousness, maybe throwing a few punches along the way, and that would be the end of it.

The corporal was prepared for almost anything. What he was not prepared for was Drew calmly opening the door and glancing his way. "Ah, there you are. I was wondering when you'd get here. Well, I surrender. Go ahead. Arrest me."

Corporal Abstinence had already dropped into battle stance, assuming that Drew had simply begun his usual villain monologue. Then the full import of the supervillain's words dawned on him. "I'm...sorry?" he said, in his darker monotone voice.

"Oh," said Drew, slightly raising his voice for the benefit of the janitor. It was a pity he didn't have a more appreciative audience. "That's right. You can't arrest me, since you're not a recognized member of law enforcement. You're a vigilante, more or less. I suppose you could do one of those citizen's arrests one hears about. Very well: do it. Snap-kick me, hit me in painful places, drag me off to your superhero headquarters, whatever. I don't care. I'm tired of fighting."

"You're pulling a Loki, aren't you?" Corporal Abstinence growled, in realization. "You're allowing yourself to be captured so you'll be able to compromise my team from within, and make us unable to stop your plan, whatever that might be."

"First, you don't have a team. You have you. Not unless you officially joined those stuffed shirts over in Rockwell. Second, I don't have a plan. I'm not a supervillain, I've got no deathtrap, no ray gun, no nothing. I'm just Drew. And maybe this is a horrible time to bring this up, but I am genuinely interested in your daughter, and I had hoped to ask your permission to-"

It really was a horrible time. Corporal Abstinence moved like lightning, flashing across the hallway, his fist closing on Drew's throat. "You..." he snarled, "stay away...from her."

"Grk!" Drew said, waving his arms, in an attempt to convey something along the lines of "Help, help, this strange man in a cape is attacking me and trying to choke me into an untimely demise!" The janitor didn't quite get all that, but he understood the main point, and he pulled out his phone. In his defense, he was in his early twenties, and he hadn't seen Corporal Abstinence, and so didn't recognize him as a genuine superhero. In fact, he was pretty sure this guy was the villain. Not only that, but he had also seen a number of movies where an ordinary civilian had bravely stood up against the bad guy despite the odds, and things had generally worked out in the movies, so he decided to try it then and there.

"You let him go!" he said tremulously. "Or I'll call 911!"

Corporal Abstinence looked at the frightened janitor, a death glare that would've sent most people screaming. The janitor, being made of sterner stuff, didn't scream. He only went very pale and then passed out. But as it happened he wasn't the only one watching the events; the apartment's security guards had seen the attack on their own monitors, and they had called the police five minutes ago. Already the corporal could hear the police sirens as they drew ever closer. He flung Drew contemptuously aside and turned to go, delivering one final death glare. "I mean it," he said. "You stay away from Meg. Or else. I will hurt you. Badly."

Then he disappeared in a dramatic flourish of grey cape.

"Sure you will," the Malevolent Med-Student said, smiling. "Sure you will."

"Muwahahahahaha!" cackled the shoulder devil. "Erm, sorry. I felt the moment was appropriate for an evil laugh."

"Don't you think I'm the one who should be giving the evil laugh? I'm the primary villain here, remember?"

"So sue me," the shoulder devil said. "Now then, let's work out what you're going to do now, shall we?"

Meanwhile, outside the apartment building, a scruffy man in a patched-through coat had just sighted Meg lying apparently unconscious on the sidewalk. He also noticed her uniform, a dark red that bore a stylized yellow mushroom cloud. The man, Bob by name, was thrilled. Superheroes, particularly unconscious or dead ones, had such wonderful toys that one could plunder from their utility belts and then sell on the black market, or use for oneself. He crept up to Meg and reached for her belt. Then a grip of iron fastened on his arm. Her eyes lit with fire. Next moment Bob was flying through the air, eventually landing safely in a Dumpster with little permanent injury, but a newfound resolve not to plunder superheroes who were apparently, but not really, unconscious.

Meg, meanwhile, had risen to her feet and taken a look around. Her jaw still ached, but no more than the pain in her heart. Her own dad had attacked her. Corporal Abstinence may have been a bit more hardcore than the captain, but she hadn't thought he had changed that much. Evidently he had. And...*Drew!*

Several different probable futures flashed through her mind. Drew could be dead. Incapacitated. Locked up somewhere. Or he might have defeated the corporal, but only by slipping back into his supervillain ways, which would mean she'd have to fight him, and that would likely put a very serious damper on their relationship. Or maybe...just as she was spinning off into even worse scenarios, the door opened and Drew himself rushed out. "Meg, are you alright?"

"Drew!" she said, trying to keep the emotion out of her voice and not quite succeeding. "I was worried, my father was going to attack-"

"He started to," Drew said, in a perfect more-in-sorrow-than-in-anger tone, like a politician about to insinuate something unpleasant about his opponent. "But then he heard the police sirens and backed off. I don't think he was very happy with our relationship, though."

"I do not think I care anymore," Meg said grimly. "I have done with Edison City. My family's gone. My own father has turned against me. I might as well stay here in Tidal."

"Meg...are you saying..." Drew said, knowing perfectly well what she was saying. She was reacting exactly as the shoulder devil had suggested she would.

"I am saying that if you were...if you wanted to..." and now she seemed lost for words.

Drew took his cue, slipping to one knee and producing a ring from his pocket. "I do want to. Margaret Case, will you marry me?"

Meg looked at him, her tear-stained face reflecting the golden light from the streetlamps, suddenly unsure. "Drew, I....I had not wanted our relationship to go like this. I had wanted us to be together with my whole family, happily ever after, just like the stories. Are you sure you want this now?"

"Absolutely," Drew said. "I know I can't replace the family you've lost, but I would very much like to build a new one. Right here, in Tidal, with me. So, will you?"

Meg closed her eyes, and then slowly nodded. "I will."

Drew smiled. The shoulder devil, who had hidden nearby behind a garden gnome, gave a sardonic round of applause. She'd suggested a lot of changes to the Malevolent Med-Student's plans, but that one she hadn't changed at all. It was positively diabolical genius.

Chapter Six

Marsha was going home late again. This time, however, she had learned from her last experience; she hadn't gone into any dark alleys or walked past any open parking lots where mutant warthogs could leap out at her. Instead she had called her friend Jill to see if she could catch a ride. For some reason Jill was unavailable, though, so Marsha had been forced to seek an alternative. She'd considered riding the city bus, but she didn't really know the routes or where they would deposit her, so instead she'd scrounged up some cash from her purse and hailed a taxi.

She'd been sitting in the backseat staring out at the houses they passed when all at once the flash of the Kaboominator had lit up the night sky. The cabbie had slammed on his brakes in astonishment, just as the shockwave hit, rocking the taxicab hard and nearly tipping it over. Fortunately it didn't, but it came down hard enough that the engine made some very foreboding sounds, and the cab wouldn't go forward again. The taxicab driver clambered out of his car and said some very insulting things at the engine; meanwhile Marsha also scrambled out of the vehicle and went for her cell phone. She'd seen explosions before ; that sort of thing was normal in Edison City. But she'd never seen anything like this. All sorts of horrific possibilities ran through her mind. Had they been nuked? Had some supervillain finally crossed the line and done something really apocalyptic? Was she going to end up dying of radiation poisoning, or worse, mutating into an uncontrollable green rage monster?

It was at that unfortunate moment that Catrina came running by. She saw Marsha standing with her phone in hand, and decided to ask directions, a reasonable idea under normal circumstances. "Excuse me," Catrina said, "but could you tell me how to get to Citrus Street?"

Catrina had momentarily forgotten that she was holding a red Sporksaber in her other hand, and that red was a color one generally associated with villains. Marsha certainly took it that way. "Ahhhhh!" she screamed in terror. She was really quite proud of that scream; just the other day her vocal coach had said that her screaming ability was first-rate, one of the best he'd seen. "Stay back! Back, you terrible person! I have a Taser, and I'm not afraid to use it!"

"You have a what?" Catrina said. "Oh, never mind. Look, I'm not a villain. I'm trying to find Super Soccer Mom, actually, so I can make her see sense. I know who blew up her house, you see. And I'm pretty sure, though not entirely, that her family's not killed. At least I hope not, because that would be unbearably tragic and...um, what is that thing and why are you pointing it at me?"

"That would be the Taser," Marsha said. "And I'll shoot you with it if you don't back off right now!"

Catrina couldn't believe what she was hearing. "Honestly, you are the absolute limit! I'm Catrina, you silly bystander! I've come in to *help* your people stop th-" But like so many people in this story she was interrupted, as Marsha fired the Taser, sending two small electrodes hurtling on a wire towards her.

But Catrina was no Asgardian deprived of immortal powers and landed on Earth; no, she had a Sporksaber, and she had been practicing swordplay since her childhood. She deflected the electrodes with almost casual ease, the blade of her Sporksaber slicing right through the wire and leaving it dangling. "Right. That was fun. Are you done now?"

Marsha very much wished she had invested in pepper spray instead. Fortunately for her, the taxicab driver had invested in something much more lethal. While Marsha had been yelling at and then attempting to Taser what she thought was a new supervillain, the cabbie had dived back into his cab, dug through the glove box, and retrieved his little friend from Smith and Wesson. He came back out and aimed the weapon right at Catrina. "Okay, drop your...." he hesitated, not sure what to call it. "Drop that. On the ground. Right now."

"Is that another, what's that word, Taser? Because the first one worked so well."

The cabbie was even more confused. "You...don't know what this is? What are you, high?"

Being unfamiliar with twenty-first century slang, Catrina took his question literally. "What does altitude have to do with anything? And no, I do not know what that is. I've time-traveled here from the 12th century; well, actually it's a bit more complicated than that, but I'd rather not go into it all just now."

Her explanation only made things worse. The cabbie had seen myriad news reports about supervillains who had come in from other time periods to wreak havoc in present-day Earth. The Time Looper, for one, had only just recently attacked Vancouver. "Yeah, well, I'm not going to tell you again. Drop that thing right now. You got three seconds."

Catrina wasn't familiar with modern tech, but she wasn't an idiot either. She had a suspicion that the black metal object he was pointing at her was going to do something unpleasant, and he seemed awfully confident that she couldn't stop it with her Sporksaber. Besides, these people were laboring under the misunderstanding that she was a villain; she clearly had to make them see that she wasn't. So she carefully deactivated her Sporksaber and set it down on the sidewalk. "There. Now then, I don't suppose we could have a calm civilized discussion like reasonable *hrk!*" She twitched rather dramatically and then fell over. It turned out that Marsha had bought one of the new sorts of Tasers which had the capacity to fire three shots before it needed to be reloaded.

"Hmph," Marsha said. "So much for you." She then dialed the police; they were extraordinarily busy of course, what with the Kaboominator and all, but once Marsha explained that the supervillain she had just tased knew something about the attack, the officer she was speaking to became infinitely more interested. Unfortunately, the officer misunderstood what Marsha was saying (her cell phone connection wasn't the greatest), and he got the impression that Catrina *was* the supervillain who had pulled off the attack. He reported that to his superiors as fast as he could. Within five minutes a squad car screeched in, followed by two more squad cars, a SWAT team, and Lucy Jackson, who had been listening to the police scanner for word on where she could help. Lucy was part of the Phenomenal Four, a support group of super-powered moms that also included Audrey. Tasha was technically part of it as well, though they hadn't gotten around to change the name yet, as she made five.

The officers and SWAT members spilled out of their vehicles and started for Catrina, but as it happened she woke up a lot faster than anyone expected. She was made of sterner stuff than the usual bad guy, and she was in a wrathful mood. Her red Sporksaber flew to her hand and ignited in a blaze of crackling energy. "I'm going to start ranting like Susan in a minute if you people don't calm down!" she exclaimed.

Others in the Phenomenal Four might have tried calm diplomacy in this situation. Audrey, for example, would have read Catrina's mind to see how much of a threat she was, and had she done that she would have realized that Catrina wasn't responsible for the attack and could be trusted, and the unfortunate events that followed might've been avoided. But Lucy was a far more practical person. "Eat lightning!" she snapped, and unleashed a powerful electric bolt right at Catrina.

The Sporksaber flashed out and caught the bolt, but the sheer force of the blast sent Catrina stumbling back a few paces. Lucy kept up the electric power, and Catrina found herself clinging to the hilt of her blade, sweat beading on her face, as she tried to hold back the lightning. She was moderately impressed with herself that she could actually do this; she'd practiced once or twice but not at this level, and not with full-fledged electric power. She wondered if there was a way she could bend it back somehow, maybe zap Lucy with her own lightning.

But she'd never have a chance to find out, because she wasn't facing amateurs. The Edison City police force wasn't one of the ones riddled with corruption or incompetence; they knew what they were about. They weren't going to simply stand back and watch while Lucy battled this new supervillain, no, they were going to take action. One of them, a newly minted officer named Bob

Lipitsky, happened to be holding a high-powered experimental tranquilizer gun; the techies in the research department had said that this one would be safe to use on people, and Bob was eager to try it out. Thus he took careful aim and fired. The dart launched from his gun with a less-than-dramatic *whiff*, impacted against Catrina's arm, and exploded in a puff of gas.

"Ow!" Catrina exclaimed. "What did you do that for?"

Lucy saw the gas, guessed what it meant, and backed off, letting the lightning die out. She wouldn't need it anyway.

"Well, alright then!" Catrina said, not sure what had happened but assuming that they had given up. "I was beginning to think you all would never listen to reason, no, instead you had to go and get all...chartreuse. Heh. That's a funny word. So is marina when you think about it. And wafting. Wafting wafting wafting." She giggled. "Um. This is odd. I'm not feeling.....turtles.....whaaaaa." Catrina collapsed into blissful unconsciousness.

"Okay, then," said the captain of the SWAT team. "We'll take it from here. Thanks for your help, Lucy, as always."

"No prob," Lucy said. "You just make sure you find out what all she wants with Tasha, you hear?"

"You bet," the captain said grimly. "She'll be singing by morning."

"Actually, sir, she might not wake up till late afternoon," Bob interjected. "The manual said this thing lasts for twelve hours or more."

"Lovely."

"Hey, y'all, I could call Audrey. She could 'path in to this girl's brain and root out something," Lucy volunteered.

The captain perked up immensely. "You do that. Have Audrey meet us back downtown, that way we'll be secure in case she wakes up prematurely, or she's got friends. You never can tell with these guys."

Dawn slowly broke over the city, spreading its golden rays over the skyscrapers and glinting off the windshields of the cars tangled up in eternal traffic jams. Tasha normally liked mornings, but not today. She hardly even noticed the rising sun as she slowly cruised over the city lines, still holding to Winston. Her face was drawn and tired, as she hadn't slept at all since she'd left Tidal. She could easily, of course, have called Audrey again and asked her friend to 'port her back, but Tasha had wanted to fly the hard way. She'd wanted time to think, to find some way to put the shattered pieces of her life back together. After long hours of watching the country roll by below her, of crying and wiping her face and crying again, of going over and over what had happened and trying to think of some way she could have stopped it, Tasha still didn't know what to do now.

Of course she wanted to find who had destroyed her home and her children. That thought remained uppermost in her mind, cold and hard as steel. But what about after that? Could she stay in the same city with Justin? Would they be able to patch things up, or had they crossed the relational Rubicon? Tasha didn't know. Worse, she had no idea how to find out, where to start. But the cold thought came back into her mind as Winston came in low towards her neighborhood. First, she had work to do. Marriage or no marriage, she was still Super Soccer Mom.

She had told Winston to block all calls, as she had very much wanted some time alone on her flight. Now she checked the readout to see if anyone had even tried to contact her. Most of the messages were from friends worrying about her safety, having seen the Kaboominator's flash and known that it had come from her neighborhood. Then Tasha saw the latest message from Lucy. Her mouth tightened into a grim line. So they'd caught someone already. Wonderful.

"Winston, take me to the police station."

The soccer ball beeped a query that meant whether she wanted to go by her home first. Tasha let out a long breath. "No, Winston, I can't. There's nothing left there. Just get me to the station."

Winston beeped again, a little mournfully, and swerved. Tasha didn't even look down at the crater as they passed over it and headed towards downtown. She closed her eyes against the smoke that still rose above it, and didn't open them again until they had touched down outside the police station. Tasha, with Winston bobbing behind her, marched inside. Fortunately Winston had passed along the news that she was coming, and Lucy and Audrey met her inside the door. Lucy hugged her friend fiercely, not saying a word. She didn't need to. Tasha understood what she wanted to say.

Audrey stood off to the side, never having been good with emotions. She waited until Lucy and Tasha broke apart. *The girl they captured is downstairs. Cell block D. They put her by herself, I think. They're not sure if she has powers;*

she didn't manifest any last night, but she might still have some, so they engaged the usual anti-power protocols.

"Great," Tasha said, her voice emotionless. "Let's go see her then."

Lucy wiped her eyes. "Yeah, girl. Let's."

They went downstairs, the warden unlocking the cell block doors and letting them pass without a word. As they went, Lucy explained about the fight, and how Catrina had been tranquilized by knockout gas. "That's why we got Audrey, so she can 'path in and see what's goin' on."

Tasha only nodded. She'd always been a bit uncomfortable with Audrey's 'pathing abilities; one never knew entirely whether one's thoughts were really private with her. But Tasha didn't much care now. She wanted to know why. And she wasn't willing to wait till the girl woke up.

She had this weapon with her, Audrey ventured as they approached her cell. She held out the deactivated Sporksaber. *It's very unusual. She said something about time-travel; I believe she may have come here from the future. I cannot be sure until I have 'pathed in.*

Tasha glanced at the Sporksaber, then back at the cell door. It was secured with an electronic keypad lock, and Lucy was about to call the warden for the code, but Tasha didn't wait. She closed her eyes, mentally interfacing with the lock. It was easier than interfacing with Winston in one respect at least; its circuitry was a lot less complicated. Within five seconds the lock beeped, and the door clanked open.

They were all three prepared in case Catrina should have woken up and sprung at them. Lightning buzzed in

Lucy's fingers. Audrey had gone into a battle-stance, ready to unleash a wave of telekinetic power. Tasha had Winston at the ready, prepared to unleash a storm of electric volts or laser fire. But they needn't have bothered; Catrina lay peacefully on her cot, a blissful smile on her face, and a tiny rivulet of drool tracing down her cheek and collecting on her pillow. They could even hear her snoring.

"Audrey?" Tasha said, gesturing to her friend. Audrey took the cue and stepped inside the cell. She could have easily 'pathed into Catrina's mind while standing outside, but when Audrey wanted to really delve into a person's subconscious, she preferred to do things a certain way. It was tradition, more than anything else. For example, she didn't really need to make physical contact with Catrina, but it was tradition for these sorts of things. She'd learned that much in 'pather school. So Audrey placed her left hand against Catrina's temple, and placed her right hand against her own. Then she closed her eyes, and focused with all her 'pathic powers.

Or at least she started to. Because at that moment the outer wall of the cell smashed into a cloud of pulverized dust, the force of the blast sending Audrey, Lucy, and Tasha flying back into the outer corridor. As Tasha leaped to her feet, she saw Titanium Walrus step through the gap in the wall, pick up the happily slumbering Catrina, and sling her ignominiously over his shoulder. "Put her down!" Tasha yelled, not out of any great concern for Catrina's welfare, but out of desperation that she would lose valuable intelligence. "Put her down right now, or so help me I will-"

"Do what, exactly?" Titanium Walrus asked, laughing. "I don't see any exploding soccer balls with you.

And I've covered all the access ports to my armor with protective lead shielding, so you can't interface in and scramble my systems!"

"Drat," Tasha mumbled to herself. This protective lead shielding business was getting to be a pain. Fortunately, she had other resources, not to mention friends. Audrey unleashed a wave of telekinetic power that sent Titanium Walrus skidding back through the hole in the outer wall of the cell. "Um, Audrey?" Tasha ventured. "I'm not sure that was such a good idea."

Oh. Sorry, Audrey apologized, as she and the others raced through the cell and outside. Titanium Walrus had already recovered himself and blasted onto his feet in the prison courtyard, firing up his jetpack.

"You morons think you can stop *me?*" the supervillain demanded, which was a tactical error since he really should've blasted off into the sky and not stopped for banter.

"Yeah, we kinda do!" Lucy said, her hand crackling with electric power.

"Well, you're wrong!" retorted Titanium Walrus in a masterful display of oratory. "You can't shoot your lightning bolts at me, or you'll hurt Catrina! My armor's shielded against lasers, so that won't work either! I've upgraded, you see, since I got out on bail!"

"How did you manage that?" Tasha asked curiously, not that she was really interested, but she wanted to encourage him in his monologuing, so as to give her friends time to work out a plan.

Titanium Walrus was about to explain all the intricate legal maneuvers employed by his lawyer to get him released on his own recognizance (a remarkable thing for a supervillain, really). But all of a sudden he felt a staggering wave of drowsiness. Audrey's voice slammed into his mind like a sledgehammer. *Go to sleep. NOW.* He didn't even pause to shut down his armor systems; he just crumpled over in a heap. He had planned for a good many contingencies, except for the one about Audrey's telepathic powers. In his defense, she didn't use them all that much in battle; she hated forcibly invading other people's minds unless absolutely necessary. Casual telepathic conversation was one thing; knocking someone unconscious was something else altogether.

    In superhero cities, the tide often turns very rapidly, and one can never be sure that the current battle has really ended. Tasha assumed that once they had taken out Titanium Walrus everything would be cool, and they could get back to the business of telepathically interrogating Catrina. But what she didn't realize was that Catrina's entrance into the story really had changed things. She had left a gaping breach in the fourth wall between her own world and the world of Edison City. Catrina wasn't the only one who had come in. And the new arrival wasn't nearly as pleasant. She had also been reading the story, having come along to the coffee shop only a little while after Catrina had read it. And she didn't much think Catrina had improved the tale at all. It was time to straighten things out herself.

    Smoke billowed in the courtyard, great dark clouds shot through with lightning. The prison PA system squawked what started out to be a warning from the warden, but suddenly got overridden by dramatic music, all drums and minor keys and ominous Latin chanting. Tasha got a very, very bad feeling about this, and she was not mistaken. For the smoke gathered itself together in a swirl of dark power, and in a flash of lightning and an ear-splitting clap of thunder it materialized into the worst possible person it could have been. It was a tall woman with dark brown hair tumbling about her face, extremely nasty-looking laser pistols held in each hand. "Tremble before me, ya twips!" she bellowed. "For I am *SUSAN!* And if you all don't hand over Catrina right this minute, I shall call down upon you all the powers of Character *Hell!*"

Tasha was suitably impressed, though she had no way of knowing that Susan wasn't in charge of Character Hell anymore. Susan did know quite a few arcane legal magics, not to mention more prosaic talents such as ways of murdering people with a spork, or a safety pin, or a Slinky. At any rate, Tasha and the others could see at once that this wasn't a poser like the Rogue Jaywalker; this was a villain not to be trifled with.

"What do *you* want with Catrina?" Tasha asked, very reasonably under the circumstances.

"I'm gonna kill her, duh," Susan said. "Been trying to do that for over a year. She has this thing about saving reality, you see, and I've been trying to wipe it out. Reality's overrated. Way. So the point being, I'm not going to recruit her or turn her loose against you people; I'm just going to shoot her right through the head. Blam. And then I'm going to make sure she jolly well *stays dead*. I don't want her resurrected by a golden spleen, or sent back from Character Heaven, or escaping from Character Hell. This time she's going to die and she's going to stay that way! Do you understand me?"

"Not terribly, no," Tasha said. "And I especially don't understand why you're trying to kill her, when she's on your side. She blew up my house, she killed my..." and here she paused, her voice faltering. Tasha regained her composure in an instant, her face tightening into a grey cold mask. "She killed my family. Destroyed my marriage. I would very much like to have words with her about that."

She expected Susan to remonstrate with her, or make some sort of demand. What she didn't expect was for the uber-villain to break down laughing. "Catrina? Catrina killed your marriage? Oh this is beautiful! Perfect! You twips! You brainless hysterical twips!" Susan giggled madly. "Really! Catrina! Killing your marriage! Oh man, this is the funniest thing since-"

But she never got to say what might've been funnier than that, because Tasha wasn't at all amused. Neither was Lucy as it happened, and she promptly expressed her irritation by unleashing a massive lightning bolt that sent Susan flying back against the prison courtyard wall. Susan scrambled upright, snarling viciously. "You wanna play that way? *Fine!*" She leveled her laser pistols and opened fire, sending a storm of plasma bolts blazing across the courtyard. Blossoms of flame shattered the prison walls and sent Tasha and the others diving for cover. Audrey dropped down, rolled quickly, and came back up in time to fire off a telekinetic power blast at Susan. To her shock and horror, Susan raised a hand and deflected it with her own power blast. "Dude, I was the mistress of all Character Hell, remember? I've got all kinds of evil powers! And don't even try that 'pathic crap on me, alright? That only works on the weak-willed, and baby, I am anything *but* weak-willed! Oh, incidentally, *corpus juris secundum!*"

With those dread words a shower of legal encyclopedias rained down from the skies and formed a high wall between the superheroines and Susan. By the time they cleared past it, Susan had gone, and Catrina had gone with her. Titanium Walrus was staggering woozily to his feet. "Wha...?"

Audrey blasted him into unconsciousness again with a flick of furious 'pathic power. Tasha very nearly used an expletive, something she never did. She couldn't believe this. She had been within moments of finding out why she had lost her family, and now she'd lost her chance. At least she'd gotten a name, though. Susan and Titanium Walrus had referred to the girl as Catrina. She was probably on record somewhere. Tasha summoned Winston. "I need a record search. Catrina, or maybe Katrina. Use both spellings. Match with her physical appearance. Find me something on her. *Anything*. And then see if you can track down this Susan as well."

Winston beeped in acknowledgment, its circuits whirring as it warmed to its work. Then it informed her that she had an incoming call. She checked the readout, not wanting to talk to Justin just yet; that wound was still too painful. Fortunately, it appeared to be Meg. Tasha answered it quickly, moving away from the others, who had set about cleaning up the courtyard and trying to explain what had happened to the prison officials.

"Mom," came Meg's usual low voice. "I think there is something you should know. Drew asked me to marry him last night. I said yes."

Tasha was taken aback. "You....Meg, are you *sure*?"

"I am. Drew is not what my father thinks he is. He is a good person. He has changed. And I love him."

"I see." Tasha didn't, really. It was all going too fast. Everything seemed like it was collapsing around her.

Meg was the only family she had left, not counting Justin, and now... "So...when..."

"Soon. Possibly today. There's a justice of the peace here in Tidal; Drew's trying to get an appointment. I called because I really wanted you out here to be with us, if you could."

"And what about..."

Meg's voice went hard. "He's not invited. I never want to speak with him again."

"Meg," Tasha said softly. "Are you sure you're not rushing into this? Are you *certain*?"

"I am. I cannot be alone right now. I need him, Mom. You don't understand."

"I just might," Tasha said. She let out a long sigh. "Just tell me when you get your appointment. I'll leave here as soon as I can, and I'll try to be there in time. I can't promise. You know how things are."

"The never-ending battle, I know," Meg said. "I will call when I hear from Drew. And Mom...I...I really hope you can make it."

"I'll try," Tasha said. The line went dead then, which was a bit odd, since Tasha would've expected Meg to say some sort of goodbye; she usually did. But Meg was under a lot of stress right now, as were they all. Tasha had never imagined her oldest daughter's wedding to be like this. She had thought it would be in a church, with Pachelbel's Canon in D and a small dimpled flower girl and all the proper traditions and ceremonies. Not like this. Not after...Tasha's knees buckled, and she sank to the broken-up ground of the courtyard, sobbing for the first time since she had learned what had happened to her family. Audrey and Lucy saw her and rushed to bring comfort. Even Winston offered a mournful beep.

Chapter Seven

Corporal Abstinence had flown back to Edison City, grimly determined to find out who had blown up his house and destroyed his family, taking his marriage with it. He hadn't reflected on the irony that Tasha was doing the same thing, more or less; had their paths crossed, perhaps things might have been different. But unfortunately the corporal hadn't been able to start his own investigation right away, as he'd been forced to assume his secret identity and deal with the aftermath of the explosion.

Justin spent the whole day filing insurance reports, talking to police and FBI investigators, and making arrangements for a place he could stay while things got sorted. The city had a department for exactly such situations as this; it had been organized back when when the city leaders realized they needed a permanent cleanup organization equipped to handle disasters on a superheroic scale. Thus was born ECARB: the Edison City Apocalypse Resolution Bureau. ECARB was pretty well funded, all things considered, and so they had enough to pay for Justin to stay in a decent hotel, until he could see about either rebuilding or buying another house. Justin put off the agents' long-term queries; he honestly didn't know what he was going to do. If he could somehow get back together with Tasha, then he could see about buying another house, but until then it would just be too much for one person. The agents realized that they were treading on awkward ground here, and withdrew.

That night Justin settled in to his small hotel room with its single bed, popped open a soft drink can, and turned on the television. Wendy Day breathlessly recapped

Catrina's capture, and her subsequent escape from the Edison City penitentiary. It was widely assumed that Catrina was in league with both Titanium Walrus and Susan, although no one knew yet who Susan was. Justin's eyes narrowed as he processed the report. There was something very strange about all this, something that bothered him immensely. Then it clicked.

Why hadn't they used the Kaboominator to break Catrina out of jail? Titanium Walrus had used his usual assortment of explosives, and it seemed Susan had been armed with laser pistols, although where she had obtained those no one could say; laser tech was still relatively new and tightly regulated. But the Kaboominator would've been powerful enough to blow right through the walls and demolish the whole prison. Indeed, the corporal wondered why they had bothered to rescue her at all. Supervillains weren't usually the loyal type; oh, sure, minions would happily rescue their villains, and there were some cases where a villain had done the same for a particularly useful minion: the Malevolent Med-Student and Candystriper sprung to mind. But rarely did supervillains bail out each other. Not without a catch, anyway. The supervillainy business was just too competitive.

Perhaps Susan and Titanium Walrus were working for Catrina? Corporal Abstinence dismissed that thought; Titanium Walrus might take a job for another villain, if he were paid well enough, but somehow Susan didn't seem like the mercenary type. She seemed more like the kind of villain who would cheerfully ignore the usual villain rules. If she'd had the Kaboominator, she most certainly would have used it. So that brought him back to the original question: where was the Kaboominator?

"Find the Kaboominator," the corporal mused aloud, "and we find the people who used it." Even if it had gotten lost somehow, there would be fingerprints. DNA traces. Something they could use. The next question, naturally, was how he could go about finding the Kaboominator. Corporal Abstinence closed his eyes, thinking hard. He remembered reading an intelligence report Mr. Acidic had copied him on, back when the Kaboominator had first been invented. Everyone had thought it used atomic technology, but apparently it didn't; instead, the fearsome device was powered by a previously undiscovered crystal that had been dug up in the deepest caves of darkest Peru. They called it Padamantium, as the crystals were exactly the same color as the marmalade one might use for a sandwich, if one were a bear that liked marmalade sandwiches. Unfortunately, when the crystals turned out to be tremendously resonant and capable of producing immense energy, several supervillains had gotten the idea to use them for something a lot worse than making marmalade sandwiches. Thus, one of them had invented the Kaboominator.

The thing was, since the padamantium crystals did give off a unique resonant signature, they could be tracked, if one had the right equipment for it. The corporal needed Tasha for this; Winston had a padamantium-tracking widget he was sure, and....not for the last time did Justin stop and catch himself; he had momentarily forgotten that he wasn't really married anymore. Every time this happened it was like a fresh blow. The corporal was beginning to wonder if he would ever get used to it.

But he'd have to get used to it pretty quick, he resolved; he couldn't just sit around moping while the

Kaboominator was unaccounted for. So he couldn't use Winston. Okay. Even as Corporal Abstinence he'd still had a few resources. True, he wasn't a multi-millionaire like Mr. Superlative, but he'd had contacts. He hadn't kept up as much with his sources in the city's underworld since he'd become the far sunnier Captain Happily Married, but he hadn't forgotten them completely.

Justin donned his grey cape, and slid open the hotel room window. He turned off the TV before he left, not wanting to waste energy and disturb the other hotel occupants, then with a dramatic flourish, he soared away into the night. It was time to go to work.

Dr. Ariel Adams was perplexed. She honestly didn't encounter amnesia cases very often, despite what people might have thought. Whenever she went home for holiday dinners, her family always asked her what it was like working in a superhero city hospital, and invariably someone asked if she'd seen a hero lose their memory and turn evil, or get brainwashed and turn evil, and whether a whack on the head really cured it. Ariel always had to patiently explain that no, amnesia didn't work that way, and hitting someone over the head was not a recommended medical practice at all. She had even written a paper on it when she was in med school. Of course, whenever she brought up med school she had to explain that no, she hadn't been in the same class with the Malevolent Med-Student, and no, she didn't know where he had studied. It had gotten to where she dreaded the holidays.

But what was confounding her on this warm summer night was that here was a genuine case of amnesia. The poor young woman who had been brought into the hospital the night before claimed that she really couldn't remember her name or anything else. Dr. Adams had treated her other injuries; she had been badly hurt, with a concussion and myriad scrapes and bruises. Then the doctor had run various tests, and had been horrified by what she had found. The poor girl had traces of all sorts of unusual pharmaceuticals in her system, some of which Dr. Adams didn't even recognize. Still and all, she didn't think any of them would serve to wipe out the patient's entire memory. They might make her a little on the eccentric side, to be sure, but not like that. Dr. Adams wondered what this girl had been doing. She didn't recognize her, but then, Dr. Adams didn't keep up overmuch with the city's eternal super-powered battles. A lot of them didn't use her hospital anyway; either they had their own health-care facilities, or they healed naturally, or they didn't want to risk exposing their identity. After all, someone would have to make the insurance co-pay.

Dr. Adams sighed wearily, and went to get a cup of coffee from the vending machine down the hall. She had developed an acquired taste for hospital coffee; granted, it wasn't anywhere near Starbucks level of quality but it was cheap, and readily available. She reached the vending machine and dug in her pockets for quarters. As she turned back to the machine to insert the quarters into the slot and select the kind of coffee she wanted, she saw a shadow reflected in the glass. She turned around, not terribly startled. "Right, which one are you then?" Living in a superhero town, one got used to having heroes appearing suddenly out of nowhere to ask one questions.

"Corporal Abstinence," he said in his newfound gravelly tones. "I need to know if you've treated anyone with trace elements of padamantium poisoning. They would've come in last night." The problem with the Kaboominator's power source was that it wasn't quite properly shielded, and so the padamantium tended to irradiate anything or anyone around it.

"Pada-what?" the doctor inquired. "I don't think I know that one. I've got several patients brought in last night, but..." she considered. Whatever this was, could it possibly be responsible for erasing her patient's memory? "I don't suppose you have information on the composition of, what did you call it?"

"Padamantium. And no, I'm afraid I don't. I'd assumed you people would."

"Yes," Ariel said, "well, I do have one patient whose system has a few things I don't recognize. I'd meant to run some more tests; I'll go and get started on those right away and let you know."

"Who is it?" the corporal demanded.

Here the doctor was in a bit of a quandary. Ordinarily she couldn't disclose confidential information about her patients to anyone other than relatives or other authorized persons. But if her patient turned out to be a supervillain, then shouldn't she help the corporal stop whatever evil plan was going on? Of course, perhaps the patient wasn't a supervillain, perhaps she had just gotten poisoned by this padamantium material, and the corporal was merely trying to help. Then the doctor decided that the whole issue was moot anyway, for a very simple reason. "I'm sorry, but the patient actually hasn't given me her name yet; she claims to have total amnesia."

"Does she?" the corporal said, in a voice that sent shivers down Dr. Adams' spine. "I've heard that padamantium poisoning might do that to someone, especially if it interacts with other chemicals. Shorts out their neural patterns, so to speak."

Dr. Adams made up her mind. "Then you should probably come and see if you recognize her. For all I know she's one of you people who got in a bit of trouble."

The corporal followed her down the corridor to the room where the patient lay. Dr. Adams opened the door and poked her head in; it looked like her patient had gone off to sleep. Dr. Adams was a bit worried about this; she'd been reluctant to prescribe medications until she was entirely certain what exactly the patient had in her system, so she had given only the basic pain meds, not something narcotic like morphine. It seemed the patient had drifted to sleep anyway, which might bode well for her recovery.

Then the corporal looked in and saw her. His mouth tightened into a grim line, and his eyes blazed behind his grey mask. He had recognized her at once, from her overly poofy bubblegum-pink hair to the red and white uniform she wore. "Candystriper."

"Who?" Dr. Adams asked. She had a vague idea of who the city's villains were, and she was pretty sure from the scowl on the corporal's face that they were dealing with someone on the dark side, but she didn't recognize the name.

"She works for the Malevolent Med-Student."

"Oy," Dr. Adams said, "him again. I am so sick of that irresponsible, unprofessional, brainless disgrace to the medical profession. And before you ask, no I *didn't* go to school with him, and I *don't* know where he did his clinicals."

"I wasn't going to ask that," the corporal said. "I was, however, going to ask where she was found."

The doctor felt a little foolish. "Oh. Well. I'm not sure off the top of my head; let me go and check the records." She went off to the nurse's station, stopping by the vending machine to grab the coffee cup that had by now been filled up by the automatic dispenser. It looked like it was going to be one of those nights.

The nurses seemed a bit nervous looking up the information about Candystriper while Corporal Abstinence was standing there glowering; it was like working next to a thundercloud. One of them whispered to Dr. Adams if she was really sure she wanted to give the superhero the information he wanted; Dr. Adams assured her that it was perfectly fine, and that the corporal was indeed trustworthy. Her voice faltered a bit, and wasn't entirely filled with conviction, but then that was perfectly understandable; she was still wary of the dour corporal, and her caffeine rush hadn't hit yet. She also hadn't recognized him as the former Captain Happily Married; if she had, she might have reacted differently.

It turned out that Candystriper had been found at an intersection not too far off from the hospital; a passerby had seen the girl lying sprawled and broken on the sidewalk and immediately called 911. Corporal Abstinence read the address off the report and nodded somberly. "Thanks. Bye." He couldn't exactly pull the usual superhero vanishing act, being in a well-lit corridor and under the suspicious eyes of two nurses and a doctor, but he did the next best thing; he dropped a cluster of smoke pellets from his utility belt. The pellets blossomed into clouds of white gas that flooded the nurses' station, and by the time it cleared and they could see again, Corporal Abstinence had vanished. "Couldn't just walk away like a normal person, could you," Dr. Adams said in irritation. "No, you types always have to leave dramatically. Superheroes. Oy."

Just then an alarm sounded at the station, the kind of alarm that signaled a patient's IV had come loose. Dr. Adams glanced casually at the room number; of course the nurses were quite capable of handling that sort of thing, but she liked to keep an eye on events nevertheless. Then more alarms for the same room went off, indicating that the patient's heart monitor wasn't picking up a beat. Now Dr. Adams was moving, because this was getting serious, and all of a sudden it occurred to her that the room number was awfully familiar. She broke into a run, dashing down to Candystriper's room. Surely the corporal hadn't been that stupid. Surely he hadn't….but it seemed he had. IV wires dangled free, as heart monitors shrilled alarms under the mistaken impression that the person they were supposed to be monitoring had suddenly passed on. The bed itself was entirely empty. The window gaped open, and a breeze blew in from outside. Candystriper had gone. Dr. Adams was pretty certain she knew who the minion had gone with. She facepalmed. She so hated when superheroes pulled this sort of thing.

Dr. Adams naturally called the police, as any doctor would do when they suspect their patient has been carried off by a superhero. The police officer who took her call was somewhat surprised to get her call; Corporal Abstinence hadn't been heard of for years. The police department had taken a dim view of Corporal Abstinence; true, he had done wonders in the narcotics enforcement department, but they didn't entirely approve of some of his methods. For example, the commissioner really frowned upon snatching a recovering patient from her hospital bed, even if she were a minion and had a reasonable connection to the Kaboominator. The commissioner wondered where Captain Happily Married had gotten to; he really could have used the hero's help right now.

As it happened, both the police and Ariel Adams were mistaken; Corporal Abstinence hadn't carried off Candystriper. He fully intended to have a conversation with her, a conversation which was sure to involve a great many stern looks and intimidating cape flourishes, and which would probably take place in the dark. But he wanted to have that conversation when she had recovered from her amnesia; right now she wouldn't have been able to tell him anything important. Not to mention, he had a slightly more pressing matter to attend to: he needed to find the Kaboominator. A device that powerful could not be allowed to fall into the wrong hands. The paramedics' report on bringing Candystriper in had said nothing about the Kaboominator or anything like it; that meant the weapon was still out there. The corporal rushed out of the hospital and leapt into the sky, flying quickly towards the street where Candystriper had been found.

At least, he started to. In his haste to track down the Kaboominator, the corporal hadn't really paused to process what he had learned. But as he flew through the evening sky aiming towards the address off the paramedics' report, he had a moment where he could think things over. All at once several rapid conclusions tumbled together in his mind, as if he'd just filled out a logic game in a puzzle book. Candystriper was involved with the Kaboominator;

he knew that because she'd gotten padamantium poisoning from it. The Kaboominator had been used to blow up his house. Candystriper worked for the Malevolent Med-Student. Those thoughts led to an inescapable truth, a conclusion that brought Corporal Abstinence up short in midflight. The Malevolent Med-Student had killed his family. That meant Drew was responsible for wrecking the corporal's marriage. And he had taken up with Meg. Why? Only one answer.

The Corporal forgot all about the Kaboominator (a mistake, as it would turn out, but understandable under the circumstances). He grabbed for his communicator and speed-dialed Meg, even as he banked hard right and blasted back towards Tidal. Whatever else he'd lost as the Captain, at least he'd kept his supersonic flight ability.

But Meg didn't answer. He couldn't think why. Surely she would've kept her phone with her. Was she deliberately avoiding his call? But no, if she had done that, she would have let it ring for a while and eventually maybe answer, or maybe let it go to voicemail. Her phone, however, had gone straight to the recorded message she'd left asking callers to leave their name and number after the beep. That meant she had turned her phone off. But why would she have done that? He knew Meg, she always kept her phone on, unless she was in some sort of very important event where she didn't want to risk having her phone ring at an inopportune moment. An event, like, say, a certain kind of ceremony, one held in a church....the corporal snapped his communicator back to his belt and flew faster than he ever had before, impelled by sudden fear.

117

Back in Edison City, Candystriper tripped lightly, and a bit woozily, down the sidewalk. She had actually been awake earlier during all the craziness with Corporal Abstinence, and, as it turned out, she'd been lying the whole time when she had claimed amnesia. Candystriper remembered things perfectly well (more or less). She'd only said she had amnesia because Marcie, the little blue manatee that only she could see, had suggested that it would be a really good idea, because she didn't want anyone in the hospital finding out who she really was. "Like, you're absolutely right, Marcie!" Candystriper had said. Marcie had followed it up with the excellent suggestion that maybe she didn't want to stick around when Corporal Abstinence came to interrogate her. That might not be a fun-fun encounter, a proposition that Candystriper readily agreed with. So she'd disconnected her own IV and climbed out the window; fortunately she happened to be on the ground floor of the hospital.

Now, however, as she walked down the city streets, Candystriper was beginning to wonder if Marcie's suggestion had been such a good idea after all. She didn't feel *one bit* well. The world wouldn't quite stop spinning, for one thing. And she kept hearing a distant sort of ring, not the ice cream truck music she usually heard but something much more tinny and unpleasant. Furthermore, now that she had pulled off her escape, she had to face the unpleasant reality that she had no idea where to go next. Her beloved Mal-Meddie was clear across the country, and he had been distressingly vague about what she should do after she fired off the Kaboominator. He'd mentioned Jill Polarity once or twice. Candystriper's face flushed with jealousy. He wasn't planning to replace her with Jill, was he? That couldn't be. She was his devoted minion, she had fired the Kaboominator, she had helped him with his evil plans time and time again. She had her own sidecar in the Malpracticycle; she'd even decorated it with flowers and a unicorn! Surely Drew wouldn't *dare* give her unicorn away to Jill, just because Jill had helped with part of his current villainous plan. Would he?

That horrifying thought decided things. She had to go back to Tidal and find out for herself. She believed deep down in her heart that she was still the Malevolent Med-Student's minion, and she always would be, but....she had to be sure. The question was, then, how could she get to Tidal? She didn't have money for a plane. She couldn't teleport. "Marcie?" Candystriper implored. "Like, ideas?"

Marcie didn't have a clue. She contemplated her navel for a long moment, in hopes that the answer would manifest itself. Sadly, Candystriper's bellybutton was as unhelpful as her shiny blue manatee friend. Worse, her head was beginning to hurt again, pounding away as if a chorus of tiny drummers had taken up residence in her brain and were performing an all-drum rendition of Beethoven's Fifth. Abruptly she decided that she could make sure she was the Malevolent Med-Student's loyal minion later. Right now she needed to go take a nap. A nap would be extraordinarily helpful, and oh look she was in a lovely city park, with a nice stretch of neat grass just perfect for napping on. Candystriper flopped down next to a statue of Athena and was off in her own happy slumberland in five seconds.

Chapter Eight

Meg hadn't predicted that it would be like this. Whenever she had followed out the probability trees on the subject of her wedding, she had generally assumed that she would be getting married in a church, surrounded by her friends and family. She had only tangentially planned for the prospect that she wouldn't be able to get a church and she'd have to rent a gazebo in a park, but she'd never planned for being married in the small office of an elderly justice of the peace, who was still fumbling through his little book looking for the proper page. He had starting reading a few moments before, but Meg had interrupted him when she realized that he wasn't marrying her but instead advising her of the constitutional rights she was waiving by pleading guilty to a class D felony.

"Dearly beloved," the justice said finally, having thankfully reached the proper page, "we are gathered here today to join these two, Drew Smith and Margaret Case, in holy matrimony." He paused impressively. Meg wondered who was the "we" he was referring to; the only other person in his little office was Drew. She wished her mother could've been here. There was still time, of course, but Meg doubted she would come. More than likely Super Soccer Mom had been called away to fight crime or avert some sort of horrible disaster, saving a busload of orphans, that sort of thing. It happened all the time. She wondered what Drew thought, whether he would've wanted her mother there or not. He was probably just relieved that her father the corporal hadn't shown up. Meg's hand tightened on Drew's, and she leaned in closer to him as the judge went on. "Marriage, that blessed arrangement..." At least, she reflected, he was clearly enunciating the R's. There was nothing more disappointing than being married by someone who couldn't enunciate clearly.

Catrina slowly opened her eyes. She blinked several times, trying to clear away the inevitable muzziness of waking up, especially when one is waking up after having been tranquilized by knockout gas and been asleep for the better part of a day. Perhaps that explained what she was seeing. Because if it didn't, if what she was seeing was actually real, then she might have made a big mistake in coming into the story.

She was lying on a tiny platform, suspended high in the air above a pit full of snarling rabid marmosets. On one side, the platform was attached to a wall bristling with razor-sharp iron spikes. At the other end, the platform led off into an extremely thin and wobbly conveyor belt, which ran over the marmoset pit and ended in an open hatch. Catrina momentarily thought this would be a way of escape, but then she saw the flickering red-yellow light emanating from the hatchway, and realized that the belt most likely led to an incinerator. "What kind of sadistic person would set this up?" Catrina demanded. Then she heard a familiar giggle from above. "Oh. It's you. I should've known."

Susan floated in on a hovercraft, still giggling. "You know, I gotta admit, I've always held to the school of thought that you should just shoot the heroes and be done with them, but really, this complicated death trap thing is a lot more fun than people make it out to be."

Catrina sniffed. "Figures you'd sell out. I thought you were the kind of villain that broke the rules, that didn't do all the death traps and monologuing and shark-pits."

"*Marmoset* pits," Susan corrected. "Marmosets. There's a difference. And hey, I can indulge my villainous side once in a while, right? There's something to be said for tradition. Not a lot, I mean, it's still mostly stupid and impractical, but once in a while it's kinda fun. Not like you'd know, anyway, because you've got that hero stick so far up your-"

"*Susan!*" Catrina interrupted, scandalized. "This is a family novel!"

Susan quirked an eyebrow. "I'm the villain. You really expect me to be tasteful? Not to mention, what's family-friendly about being eaten alive by wild marmosets? That's like making a kid's movie where a cute little lion cub loses his father to a stampede of wildebeests and then gets tricked into thinking its his own fault by the evil uncle who murdered his father in the first place. What kind of kid's movie is that?"

"Actually, I heard there was a movie like that, and it did smashingly well," Catrina replied archly.

"*Real*-ly," Susan said. "I'll have to check that out. Meanwhile, I think it's time I explained exactly how this thing works."

"Oh joy. I can't wait."

Susan produced a portable whiteboard, which she balanced on a tripod behind her on the hovercraft, then pulled out a green marker, with which she diagrammed exactly how Catrina's demise will occur. "Right, so, I'll use really small words, and stick figures, so you'll be sure to get this, ya moron. When I push the appropriately red button, that spiky panel behind you will start moving. That means you'll have to run onto the conveyor belt in order to get away. If you fall off the belt, you'll get eaten by the marmosets. Also, once you step onto the belt, your body weight will set off a detonator that'll start a timed countdown. You have thirty seconds to make it across the belt before the dynamite I've wired to it explodes, whereupon you'll either die in the explosion, or fall off and, again, get eaten by marmosets. The belt leads to that door, which opens onto a slide that drops you right into the incinerator. I've gone over the plans the guy who built this left; there's no possible way to escape. And even if you did, it'll take some time, and that's the whole point."

"Er, I'm sorry, but I'm afraid I've lost you there," Catrina interjected. "Isn't the whole point to kill me, either by incineration or spike or death by explosives or death by marmoset?"

Susan smiled. "Oh no. See, this whole thing is just to keep you occupied. Because at this moment Meg Atomic is making a horrible life choice. She's about to get married to the Malevolent Med-Student. Which means you've got to make it to the church on time. Oh. Wait. You can't. Because in about a minute you're going to be marmoset droppings."

Catrina gasped. Meg couldn't marry the Malevolent Med-Student, not when he was responsible for breaking up her parents' marriage and killing her family (apparently). But on the other hand, Susan had a point. The deathtrap was so ridiculously complicated that Catrina would probably need a couple minutes just to sort it all out. And by the time she did eventually escape it and gotten to the church, Meg would've said her vows and taken off for the reception. Catrina might not even make it in time to catch the bouquet, which, knowing who she was marrying, would probably be laced with anthrax anyway. This was a problem.

It became even more of a problem when Susan packed away the whiteboard and flourished a small remote control, on which gleamed a bright red button. "Well, that's about all the exposition I'm in the mood for. Let's get this party started!" She pressed the button dramatically, and then pulled a lever on the hovercraft, sending it swooping up towards an open panel in the ceiling. Catrina was really very insulted; Susan wasn't even giving her the respect of staying around to watch her die; she was just taking off like any other standard two-bit supervillain leaving the corny hero to die in her elaborate deathtrap. That was just rude. Not to mention unprofessional. Then a horrible thought struck her. Maybe Susan hadn't left Catrina out of some supervillainous distaste for the heroine. Maybe Susan had somewhere to be. Somewhere like...the wedding!

Unfortunately, just as she realized this, the spiky wall panel behind her began to grind slowly forward. The marmosets below her stepped up their chattering in anticipation of a potential kill. Catrina had a very, very bad feeling about this.

The justice of the peace coughed, suddenly, pausing in his reading from his book. "Erm, I'm terribly sorry, but I've just recollected, for a marriage ceremony to be valid there needs to be two witnesses, who'll have to sign the marriage license. I don't suppose there's anyone else coming? I could call the county clerk, and I'm sure she has someone else in the office she could bring along..."

Meg sighed. This was becoming less and less like what she had always dreamed. She didn't even know the

Tidal county clerk. "I guess you should call her," she said, looking at Drew for confirmation.

"Or maybe not," said a new voice. Meg and Drew spun around, to see Super Soccer Mom standing in the doorway, smiling, though her eyes were very misty indeed. "There weren't any orphans who needed saving right now, and if there are Audrey said she would cover. I couldn't miss this."

Meg hugged her mother fiercely, not trusting herself to say anything for a moment. When they pulled apart, Tasha turned and cast a sharp glance at Drew. "Mr. Smith," she said, "I hope you really have reformed. I trust my daughter; she knows what she's doing. But..."

Drew made an elegant bow. "Ma'am," he said, "I understand what you must be going through. All I can say is that I really do love Meg, and I would guard her with my own life. I have changed, ma'am. Truly I have."

Tasha smiled guardedly. "I'll hold you to that." Then she turned to the justice of the peace. "Out of curiosity, can an artificially intelligent soccer ball serve as a witness in this jurisdiction? Winston's done that before, twice actually."

The judge hemmed and hawed a bit, before finally agreeing, not without some confusion. So Tasha signed the marriage license, and then Winston extended a pen from a panel that signed in neat script. The justice hunted up his place in his book again, and continued. "Matrimony is an honorable estate, and is not to be entered into unadvisedly or lightly, but reverently and discreetly. If anyone can show just cause why this man and this woman may not lawfully be joined together, let them speak now, or forever hold their piece."

Meg winced inwardly; she hated this part. She had read *Jane Eyre* as a child where the clergyman had made the traditional request, and someone actually had spoken up, and ever since then Meg had always worried at every wedding that the same thing would happen. True, she didn't expect that Drew would turn out to have a crazy wife still living and hiding in his attic, but there were all sorts of other possibilities. She could think of six right now, and four of them had to do with her father bursting through the door. The corporal was exactly the sort of person who *would* speak up, and he would probably have some sort of contrived legal reason why they couldn't get married, and then there'd probably be a fight, and things would go downhill from there. She held her breath, waiting for the office door to bang open and Corporal Abstinence to storm in.

To her surprise, it didn't, and he didn't. Instead, after a moment's pause, the justice went on with the ceremony, having not even looked up from the page. He had never had anyone speak up in his weddings, and he didn't expect this to be the first. "Have you the rings?" he asked, and Drew produced them from his pocket. "Right, then. Drew, would you place your ring on Meg's finger, and repeat after me. I, Drew, take you Meg, to be my lawfully wedding wife..."

As Drew repeated the immemorial words, Meg dismissed her unfortunate probabilities with a happy sigh. True, this wasn't what she had predicted, but at least her mother had made it, and maybe things would work out happily after all.

Drew finished, smiling as he slid the ring on her finger, and now it was Meg's turn. She took the little golden circlet from the justice's hand, and started to repeat her own vows. "I, Meg, take you, Drew, to be my lawfully wedded-"

The wall behind the judge exploded, pulverized in a shower of concrete dust, glass fragments, and little bits of parchment from the judge's framed law degrees. "Oh, he did *not!*" Meg exclaimed, her eyes flaming. Winston's lasers and electro-stun wires powered up, and Tasha assumed a ready for battle stance, even as she tried to come to grips with the fact that she was going to have to fight her husband for the second time in as many days. Drew, curiously, didn't seem alarmed at all. He had a small smile on his face, almost as if he were looking forward to what was about to happen.

Meg strained to see through the dust cloud, looking for the first sign of her father so she could blast him with her atomic rays. Then Winston, evidently in response to a mental command from Super Soccer Mom (who wasn't particularly in a waiting mood) opened up a fan attachment and blew the dust cloud away. Both Meg and Tasha gasped in surprise. It wasn't Corporal Abstinence after all.

Susan stood proud and defiant on her hovercraft, twin blasters aimed right at them. "Eat laser, ya morons!" she yelled, and opened fire. Winston rapidly extended a ray shield that blocked the laser bolts, just in time to deflect them from hitting the terrified justice of the peace, who had never quite gotten used to superhero combat.

"She seems new!" Meg commented to her mother.

"She is!" Tasha replied. "She's working with Catrina, the girl who attacked our house! We'd captured her, but then this girl came in and broke her out of prison!"

"Oh, *did* she?" Meg snarled in a burst of atomic fury. Her hands blazed with yellow light, and Winston obligingly dropped part of the ray shield for her. Meg fired an atomic blast straight through at Susan, only it didn't hit Susan; instead it hit a Volvo that had dropped in out of nowhere. The car instantly vaporized in a flash, but Meg had time enough to see that it had been laced with purple energy. She rapidly compared the set of superheroes who had purple energy powers, and the set who could control metal cars, but neither matched. "Hi!" Jill Polarity said, poking her head round the hole in the courthouse wall. "I'm new also, actually, I've been keeping my powers a secret, but then I met-*hrrrrrrrrk*!"

An electric stun bolt had just flown in out of nowhere and zapped Jill into unconsciousness. Everyone turned to see who had fired it. Corporal Abstinence floated grimly in the sky, his super-modified Taser of Purity held in his black-gloved hand. "Looks like the wedding's off," he said. "Pity."

Meg's emotions flared as heatedly as the atomic flames in her eyes. "Honestly, Dad! *Let. It. Go.* I am marrying Drew Smith today, and there's not a thing you or anyone else can do about it. I cannot *believe* you would come back for this, especially considering what happened the last time!"

"She makes a good point," Drew observed. "She's wrong, but if she weren't, she'd make a good point. Actually I'm not marrying her, so you can just run along, corporal, and do whatever it is you do. Tell middle-schoolers to just say no, or something. I have elsewhere to be."

Meg turned to him, her face all confusion and hurt. "What....what do you mean, you're not marrying me? I thought...I thought..."

Susan whistled to catch his attention, and tossed him a white coat through the hole in the ray shield that Winston hadn't closed yet, a white coat that was all too familiar. Drew slipped it on, smiling as if he had just reunited with an old friend. When he spoke, his voice was tense with menace. "That's your problem, Meg, m' dear. You think. Way too much. See, I was going to marry you, make sure I have legal claim to your estate, and then dispose of you and the rest of your family, but then I met Susan. And zing went the strings of my evil, evil heart!"

"Oh, Drew, baby," Susan said. "You make me feel like a villainous woman!"

The Malevolent Med-Student laughed exultantly. Then he pulled from the coat's pocket a small green cylinder. "This, you should know, is a bomb powered by a padamantium crystal I borrowed from the Kaboominator. I made it based on what you told me about subatomic theory, Meg. So, in thanks for that, I'll give you all a chance; you stand down, drop the ray shields and the Taser of Purity and your atomic hands and so forth, and let me and my new girl walk on out of here. We have things to do, people to kill, a planet to take over, all that. Or, if you don't let us go, I'll set this off. Actually, I've already pushed the detonator. If I take my hand off of the pressure pad, it'll blow in exactly ten seconds, and take all of us with it, not to mention a good portion of downtown Tidal. And what that will do to the real-estate market in this area, I shudder to think!"

Tasha looked at the corporal, and at Meg, and saw in their eyes the inevitability of the situation. They couldn't let the Malevolent Med-Student wipe out all those innocent people. So she sent a calm thought to Winston, and the ray shield lowered completely. The Malevolent Med-Student, his white medical coat flaring behind him, strode out to the hovercraft. The shoulder-devil's plan had gone splendidly. Making contact with Susan was its most brilliant suggestion yet. Drew was really beginning to like the creature, even if it was a tiny manifestation of pure evil.

Meg watched him go in stunned astonishment. "But...I thought...." she said in a quivering voice. "Drew?"

"Should've listened to your father, my dear!" the Malevolent Med-Student tossed back, as he leaped on board the hovercraft behind Susan.

"What he said!" Susan yelled. "And, by the way, just for the record, I was never working with Catrina! She was probably trying to *help* you idiots! I'd recommend you apologize, but in about five seconds it won't matter, because she'll have met one of four possible messy demises! See ya!"

The hovercraft rocketed away into the sky, trailing smoke behind it. Tasha turned to comfort Meg, who was still standing there in the wreck of the courthouse, staring at the hovercraft's smoke trail in utter disbelief. This wasn't predictable. It didn't make sense. She had thought...she had never imagined...never..."

Then the hovercraft banked and raced back towards them. For one wild second Meg thought it had all been some sort of trick, that Drew was working deep undercover and maybe he'd set up this whole thing to get Jill and Susan captured. But then the hovercraft flew overhead, and the Malevolent Med-Student leaned out and waved. "Oh, I almost forgot, I didn't give you a wedding present! Catch!" He threw out the padamantium bomb, and then the hovercraft wheeled away again, racing off at a considerably faster rate than it had been. The bomb tumbled down, and then thwacked right into Corporal Abstinence's outstretched hand.

"Winston can disarm it," Tasha said, running towards him, "or I can 'path in!"

"No time," the corporal said. "Not even you can do that in the time it's got left. I'll have to fly it out."

"But..."

The corporal looked at Tasha for a second that seemed to them like an eternity. "I do love you, Tasha. Always have." She started to say something, her eyes fixed on his, but then he shot skyward, flying supersonic, racing towards the clouds. Seconds later a hellishly bright flash lit the skies above Tidal.

Catrina saw the flash distantly, through the open ceiling panel. She knew that couldn't mean anything good, and the plot of the story had likely gone horribly wrong. Susan must have done something terrible. She had to get out of this, somehow. But she only had a few seconds at most before the spikes reached her, and then she'd have to risk the booby-trapped conveyor belt above the pit of marmosets, and if she survived that then she would wind up being incinerated. If only she had her Sporksaber!

Then all at once, in her moment of greatest peril, Catrina had a flashback. She remembered all the way back to when she was a small child practicing with her very first pointy stick (she hadn't quite gotten to swords yet). She had broken the stick by hitting it against a big rock too hard, whereupon the little three-year-old Catrina had responded with all the wisdom and maturity of her age; she flung down the broken stick and burst into tears. Her mother (this was before she'd gotten murdered by Vladimir the Marauder and then resurrected by Catrina) had run out and assured her distraught daughter that everything was okay, that she didn't need a pointy stick to be a princess.

Her words flashed through Catrina's mind, and she smiled her trademark slow smile. She didn't need a pointy stick to be a princess. She was a princess with or without weapons, because deep down she believed in herself and in the story, and so that meant that if she were a princess, she could do anything a standard princess could do. And it was a matter of faith that all princesses could summon cute woodland animals to do their bidding. Catrina opened her mouth and sang some very tuneful syllables. "Lalalaaaaaa, la la la la laaaaaaaa..."

The marmosets below her perked up. She sang more rapidly, then broke into a quick rendition of her theme song, the tune of which she'd appropriated from Wagner. "I'm Catrina, I am a princess, I don't kill wabbits, that's not what I doooooo! I'm Catrina, this is my theme song, I don't like Susan, neither should youuuuuuu!" Catrina was about to launch into the second verse, but at that moment the spikes reached her, and she rushed forward in sudden panic onto the conveyor belt. She heard a click and then rapid beeping, and she glanced down to see if her song had worked on the marmosets, only at that moment she lost her balance, tripped, and fell off the belt, plunging down towards them, in a very dramatic cliffhanger and an excellent place in which to end this chapter.

Chapter Nine

Catrina squeezed her eyes tight shut as she fell; if it hadn't worked and the marmosets were going to tear her to bits with their razor-sharp teeth, she really preferred not to watch. Then she landed, but on not sharp pointy teeth, no, she landed on something soft. Soft and...*furry!* Catrina's eyes flew open, and she saw that the bedazzled marmosets (who really were quite cute when they weren't trying to tear her into tiny bits) had gotten together and linked their arms, catching her very neatly. The conveyor belt exploded above her, and Catrina breathed a sigh of relief. Her princess skills had worked after all. "Well, hey," she said, "good show, you chaps. Now, I don't suppose you could get me out of here without going through the incinerator door?"

The marmosets consulted, and assembled into a marmoset chain that piled up towards the open ceiling panel out of which Susan had flown. Together they lifted Catrina up, past the wall spikes and the incinerator door, and hoisted her right through the panel into the open air. Catrina glanced about; it took her eyes a few seconds to adjust to the dark, but she saw that she was standing on the roof of a large abandoned warehouse, surrounded by a lot of other warehouses; it seemed they were in Tidal's industrial district. "Naturally," she sighed. "These villains have no imagination. It's always the abandoned warehouse or the hidden base in the volcano. Oh well." She waved a cheery goodbye to the marmosets. "Bye, you all! Have fun...doing...whatever it is that marmosets do." With that, she set off, in hopes of finding out what on earth had gone wrong with the story. Catrina felt a bit guilty about all that; she had never meant to bring Susan into the story along with her. "Right, this is the last time," she promised herself. "From now on I'll stick to my own story and leave everyone else's alone. Absolutely. The last time. Ever."

But first, she knew, she would have to undo the harm she had done. The only way for her to do that was to track down Susan. She stopped and considered; Susan had been going to Meg's wedding. So Catrina still needed to get herself to the church on time. But would Meg actually be getting married in a church? She was marrying the Malevolent Med-Student, after all; surely most pastors would be reluctant to conduct a supervillain wedding. But suppose she were going for a civil marriage.... "The courthouse!" Catrina said, in an impressive burst of deduction.

It didn't take her all that long to find the courthouse, mainly because she practically stopped a policeman and asked for directions. The policeman was so tickled by this (he'd never had anyone ask him directions before, since they all used GPS or online maps nowadays) that he offered her a ride to the courthouse in his squad car. He explained that he was going there anyway, as police from across Tidal were being called in to deal with the aftermath of a supervillain attack. "Someone from Edison City tried to blow the place up!" he explained. "But it's someone new, apparently, not the usual cape and cowl brigade."

Catrina scowled. "Let me guess. It's a woman, brown hair, name's Susan, carries two laser pistols, and uses frightful language."

"That's her exactly, ma'am," the police officer said in surprise. "How'd you know?"

"We've met before."

"Oh?" the police officer said, his voice becoming considerably more guarded. "And when exactly was that, ma'am?"

Catrina could not believe this. "Honestly: is *everyone* in this story going to assume I'm working with Susan?"

"You're working with Susan?" the police officer said, jumping rapidly into an entirely wrong (though understandable) interpretation of her words. "Ma'am, I'm afraid we might need to continue this conversation downtown."

"Which is where we're going anyway," Catrina pointed out.

"Oh," he said, as he had honestly forgotten this in the excitement of the moment. "Good point."

"You're not going to arrest me, are you? Because I've already done that once on this trip, and I'd rather not go through that again. Getting hit by, what do you call it, a Taser, wasn't exactly a fun-fun experience." Catrina was really saying a bit too much at this point, but then she had little experience with modern law enforcement, and she was woefully ignorant of her Fifth Amendment right against self-incrimination. She might've had a decent legal case, as she hadn't yet been given her Miranda rights, but on the other hand a hypothetical prosecutor would argue that she hadn't been placed in custody; she hadn't been handcuffed or restrained, or even gotten inside the police car yet. At any rate, all of this became a moot issue, because the policeman was very well aware of the niceties of Constitutional criminal procedure. "I'm afraid I am, miss," he replied, producing a pair of handcuffs. "You have the right to remain silent and refuse to answer any questions. Do you understand?"

"Er, no, I don't. First, isn't remaining silent and refusing to answer any questions a bit redundant?" Catrina wasn't a law student, or she would have realized that the legal world is just full of redundancies that make little sense unless one really gets into the nuance of the situation. "Second, that sounded awfully canned. Is this a speech of some sort that you're required to make?"

The policeman was taken aback. He was fairly new on the force, but he had still arrested a decent number of criminals; some of them protested their innocence and some swore violent revenge (those were usually the wannabe supervillain types), but he had never before encountered someone like this. "Well...yes...it's your Miranda rights. I'm supposed to tell you so you won't feel intimidated into confessing to something you didn't commit."

"Oh," said Catrina. "How helpful. And you're supposed to tell me this because someone named Miranda said you should?"

The policeman then attempted to explain about *Miranda v. Arizona*, but this soon launched into a discussion of the Fifth Amendment, which required explaining the Constitution, which then blossomed out into a full-blown discussion of democracy. Catrina was thunderstruck by what she was hearing. She had come, one must remember, from the 12th century, where she had been a princess in a castle ruling her people by divine right (technically her parents ruled them, of course, but Catrina would have to take over eventually). She had never dreamed of a system where the people actually got to choose their leaders. "But...suppose they pick the wrong person?"

The police officer had started as a political science major in college, and he'd had a good many discussions exactly like this before he'd switched to criminal justice. He assumed that Catrina was from some tiny East European country like Plaznik that maybe hadn't gotten to the whole democracy trend yet. Warming to the debate, he forgot all about the fact that he was supposed to be arresting her. "Well, that's their decision, then!" he said. "But at least they get to pick, and if they don't like who they've elected then they can always remove them in the next election. But suppose some princess's people decide they don't like her. They can't get rid of her as easily as that, can they? They'd have to launch a revolution, and those get awfully messy."

"My people wouldn't start a revolution," Catrina retorted hotly. "They like me!"

"Are you sure?" the policeman challenged. "You ever ask them? You ever even think about it?"

"Well...no...not exactly..."

"There! You see? You don't even know. Now, in America, we have elections and political commentary all the time, and people get to express exactly what they think of their leaders, and yeah, sometimes it gets a bit messy and people get in arguments about it, but we don't have to start revolutions or resort to violence to settle our political differences!"

He knew he was probably oversimplifying things; if Catrina was still trying to grasp the basic premise of democracy, she probably wasn't ready for a discussion about federalism, counter-majoritarian difficulties, and checks and balances. Unfortunately, Catrina was a little more sharp than he'd given her credit for. "So you settle everything peacefully, do you? It's all civility and reasoned discussion, is it?"

"Exactly!" the policeman said, a bit optimistically.

"So tell me: why is it that from the moment I set foot in this very reasonable and civilized society, I have been shot with a Taser, tranquilized, nearly thrown to a pit of wild marmosets, and now I'm about to be arrested and taken off to prison. And that's just *this* trip! The first time I came here I nearly got arrested too, because some jerk insulted my mother in a most distasteful way, and naturally I had to slug him. And they were going to arrest *me*! Oh, sure, they didn't, but only because I turned into a zombie penguin. But still. How civilized is that?"

The policeman grew heated in his turn. "Just because we're democratic doesn't mean we're perfect; no country is! But we're a whole lot better than some monarchy where no one ever gets to pick who leads, and where the king can do anything he likes and get away with it. We fought a revolution over that!" Again he knew he was oversimplifying, but he was getting upset; he'd assumed this sort of thing was understood pretty well everywhere.

"Did you?" Catrina said. "And everyone's been happy and civilized ever since?"

"Well, no, like I said, nobody's perfect, we did have a civil war and all, but since then we've-"

Catrina's eyebrows shot upward in mock surprise. "Oh-*ho!* But I thought democracy meant everyone could remove their leaders peacefully if they didn't like them! You mean that didn't work?"

The policeman was about to explain what the Civil War had been about, and why Catrina's understanding of democratic theory was very much mistaken. Unfortunately in all this time they had forgotten that they were standing in an area of town that wasn't entirely safe, and was prowled both by ordinary civilian criminals and supervillains bent on evil schemes. One of them was the Rogue Jaywalker, who had decided to start over in Tidal after his humiliating defeat by Captain Happily Married. He saw the two arguing and noted that neither appeared to have weapons ready to hand. Perfect, he thought. He would take out the police officer and then order the woman to hand over her money, jewels, and other valuables. Standard mugging, no problem. What could possibly go wrong?

He should've learned never to ask that question. Because even as he reached for his gun to commence the mugging, a dart hummed in and hit his head, puffing out into a white flower. The Rogue Jaywalker had about two seconds to realize that something had indeed gone wrong before his eyes glowed red, and he wasn't thinking anymore.

"Meh, heh, heh, heh," chortled Admiral Zombie Lady, who'd snuck up behind him. Her Zombification Dart-Thrower had worked. She was so pleased. Of course, this wasn't the first time she'd used it; she had tested it on several superheroes already, and it had performed smashingly, but this was the first time she'd fired it out in the field. Now she knew it worked. "Right," she said, "you. Go....oh, I don't know, do something bad. But not here. Some other rundown suburb with people ripe for mugging. I'll handle things here, thank you."

The Rogue Jaywalker stumbled off, unaware that he was being grossly mislabeled; a true zombie is someone who's died and been brought horribly back to life by a virus or some other thing; all he qualified for was a mind-controlled minion. Admiral Zombie Lady hadn't done her research, though, and she had never read any zombie literature. So, rather than thinking over her misdeeds, she simply fired the Zombification Dart-Thrower again, this time right at Catrina. Worse, this time she fired the flower that had the earbud attachment, so she could give Catrina orders secretly from the shadows.

Catrina twitched as the dart hit her head and puffed out into its diabolical flower. Then her eyes glowed red. "I must attack the policeman," she said, and immediately snap-kicked him so hard that he flew several feet backward into a trash can. The officer scrambled to his feet and went for his gun, but the power of Catrina's snap-kick had knocked it clean from his holster (he hadn't properly secured it in there anyway, a very serious mistake). Catrina had caught it in midair and aimed it at him. Then she repeated what Admiral Zombie Lady told her to say. "Run. Go back to your pathetic police department and tell them that I am Catrina, and I am going to destroy your world."

The officer dutifully ran, and Catrina watched him go. Admiral Zombie Lady emerged from the shadows, and gave her new minion a deceptively friendly pat on the back. "Well done, C. Now then, let's get you back to Blackacre, shall we? I've got a delivery to make."

It turned out that Admiral Zombie Lady had a hovercraft of her own (there had been a sale on hovercrafts at Villain-Mart that year). She carefully steered it out of Tidal and over the moonlit Pacific, keeping careful watch on her navigational system. Finding the Malevolent Med-Student's island lair could be tricky, as he'd somehow managed to keep it off Google Maps and Mapquest both. She had to go by exact longitude and latitude coordinates, and even then it was protected by an energy shield, which meant she would have to signal to be let in. "Here, you," she said to Catrina, "make yourself useful. Keep this thing flying while I double-check the coordinates."

Catrina soundlessly took the wheel. Unfortunately there was a small problem with Admiral Zombie-Lady's Control Flowers; they allowed her to control people as her hapless minions, all right, but they didn't give the minions any more knowledge than they already had. Catrina in her non-zombified state had absolutely no idea about how to fly a hovercraft. The Control Flower called up a memory from the last time she had flown anything, and remembered that mainly what she had done was frantically push a couple of buttons. So she did. With one hand holding the wheel, she reached out and pushed the nearest buttons that caught her eye. The first button she pushed locked in the autopilot on course to Blackacre, which was an awfully lucky thing, since the second button turned out to be the ejector-control for Admiral Zombie Lady's seat. The supervillain didn't even have time to realize what had happened before she tumbled out of the hovercraft, and landed with a splash in the ocean, twenty feet away from a passing Coast Guard cruiser. Admiral Zombie Lady's night would just get worse from there.

Having successfully followed orders (more or less), Catrina sat back in her seat and waited for further instructions, but those would be less than forthcoming, as Admiral Zombie Lady was currently yelling very impolite things at the Coast Guard sailors. So without further orders, Catrina just waited quietly, as the hovercraft flew steadily on into the west, heading right for Blackacre.

Inwardly, Catrina was positively fuming. She had been through a lot of indignities in her existence: she'd been killed and resurrected multiple times, she'd been made a magenta-colored ghost, she'd been cloned, she'd been dematerialized and rematerialized elsewhere as a fetching shade of violet, she'd been miniaturized and teleported inside a person's mouth, and she had been forced to listen to three hundred million and one playings of Rebecca Black's "Friday". In this story alone she had been tasered twice, tranquilized, kidnapped by a supervillain, nearly messily devoured by wild marmosets, and then mistaken for a villain by a number of well-meaning but idiotic citizens. But this, this was the absolute limit.

She had been possessed once, by the vengeful spirit of Susan which Catrina had inadvertently invoked by calling on the fictional Calormene god Tash, but she'd kicked Susan out again and retaken herself without undue delay or harm to those around her. The worst thing Susan had done while possessing Catrina had been to discover the magic sword Continuityslicer and change Catrina's name, and that hadn't worked out so badly; Catrina had gotten used to her name and rather fancied it. But now she wasn't even being controlled by a competent supervillain; she had fallen victim to Admiral Zombie Lady, who couldn't even use the word "zombie" correctly, let alone take basic precautions that would prevent her from being ejected from her hovercraft by her own minion. Now Catrina was stuck, her body still running on autopilot as locked-in as the hovercraft's own system, her mind trapped inside herself. She hated when the bad guys did this: opening up her brain and playing around inside. They never played elegant games either, games that called for thought and strategy like chess, for example. Catrina was quite good at chess and enjoyed it very much, so she wouldn't have cared too badly if she'd been made a pawn on some evil grandmaster's chessboard. But the game the bad guys seemed to be playing now had all the poetic elegance of mud wrestling, with Catrina as the mud. She didn't much care for that at all.

The trouble was, she couldn't see much of anything she could do about it. It wasn't like she had an alternate personality in her body she could kick out by mentally blasting Friday at them. Admiral Zombie Lady's Control Flower had gone right past the mind, apparently, and jacked into her body's nervous systems, essentially making her no more than a robot. "But did she call herself Admiral Robot Lady?" Catrina demanded, though naturally no one could hear. "Noooooo! Of course not! Honestly."

She tried all she could think of, willed herself to move as hard as she could, but nothing worked. Catrina's body sat there obstinately in the co-pilot's seat, as unresponsive as if it were dead. This was even worse than being a ghost; as a ghost Catrina could at least float around and wave her arms in appropriately spectral fashion. All she could do now was think. That, and observe; whatever else the Control Flower had done to her, it hadn't completely deprived her of her senses. She could still see and hear things, though she couldn't do zip about what she saw and heard. But if all she could do was observe, then she would observe with all her might and main. Maybe she could get a clue as to who was responsible for all this. It clearly wasn't Admiral Zombie Lady; she had obviously been making a delivery to someone. Was she working for Susan? Maybe, but Catrina wondered whether Susan had really been in the story long enough to work her way into a position of power. On the other hand, she had managed to blast into the city jail, carried off Catrina, and then left her in a ridiculously complicated deathtrap. Had she set that up herself, or had she just appropriated someone else's deathtrap? Susan wasn't above cheating when she had to, and Catrina had learned long ago never to underestimate her nemesis. She wouldn't be at all surprised if Susan had teamed up with the story's proper villain: the Malevolent Med-student. That would be just like her.

With these thoughts in mind, Catrina kept on observing as the hovercraft flew on. The scenery wasn't much to write home about, even if Catrina had been in possession of her corporeal form long enough to write anything. All she could see was an unending stretch of blue-green water, and the occasional seabird, badly startled to find a hovercraft zipping past it. Once or twice Catrina saw a ship in her peripheral vision, and she would've liked to see further, but to her exasperation her zombified form wouldn't even turn her head. Catrina was stuck looking straight forward. She supposed she should be grateful; if her body had closed its eyes, she'd be in for a lousy time indeed.

Hours upon hours went by, and the sun slowly dipped towards the horizon and got in her eyes, and still she saw nothing of interest. Even the seabirds died out. Catrina might have found that ominous, if she hadn't still been glowering about her unpleasant predicament. Then all at once a dark mass loomed up in her field of vision. Catrina mentally gasped in surprise. They had arrived at last! The secret villain lair! The place where Admiral Zombie Lady had been going to make her delivery of the Zombification Dart-Thrower! And....it's a volcano, Catrina realized in disgust. Always the volcano. Supervillains had no imagination anymore.

To make matters worse, it wasn't even an active volcano. As the hovercraft swooped in and made a slow circle around the mountain's sheer black cone, Catrina noted the absence of any smoke trails, fresh grey ash, or signs of any recent lava flows. The volcano didn't seem to have been going in years, if it ever had. Worse, there wasn't any other sign of friendly life on the island. Catrina couldn't see any trees, any cool ponds or impenetrable jungles in which she could hide, if she could manage to regain herself and make an escape. The whole thing was stark rock, black and barren, sloping down from the volcano to desolate beaches where no ship could safely land. The only sign of human activity she could see was the occasional glinting steel of the barrels of guns set in rocky outcroppings. Catrina's opinion of the island as a villain base ticked slightly upward. The place had clearly been fortified and well-defended. Anyone coming against it from the sea or air would have a nasty time taking it.

The hovercraft, having finished its circle around the volcano, now came to a rest, floating just outside a thin cleft in the mountain's sheer obsidian side. The radio buzzed sharply, startling Catrina, who had gotten used to the silence in the hovercraft during its long flight. "Identify yourself and state your business here." The tone was terse and commanding; whoever was behind it would clearly brook no nonsense. Catrina started to respond, then mentally facepalmed. Now the true horror of her predicament became clear. She would've loved to identify herself, either with a fake name and trying to con her way into the volcano fortress somehow, or maybe with her real name in a bold springing of the trap the bad guys had set for her. But she couldn't do anything. She could only listen in mounting aggravation as her body sat there staring at the hovercraft's windshield, while the radio crackled with increasingly strident demands. When they started mentioning anti-aircraft fire, Catrina's irritation blossomed into panic. She was going to get blown up, she just knew it, and if she weren't vaporized in the first volley then she'd end up plunging into the ocean and drowning, or else getting horribly splatted against the rock of the island. Great, she thought. I'm going to die. Again. This is what, the sixth time? Seventh maybe? She had honestly lost count. As the voice on the radio launched into a ten-second countdown, Catrina braced herself for yet another demise.

Chapter Ten

Kovach was a minion who knew his duty. He had read the minion handbook of instructions, issued on the first day to everyone who arrived at Blackacre, along with the free t-shirt. Kovach had actually paid attention to the parts that outlined what he was supposed to do, things like never interrupting the supervillain during a monologue, keeping the death ray guns polished, and never going off alone to investigate a strange noise. So when the hovercraft appeared on his screen, Kovach followed his handbook procedures to the letter. He demanded that the craft identify itself. When it didn't, he began the countdown. Already his hand was inching towards the red button that would unleash a salvo of flaming rockets which would blow the hovercraft into tiny bits. Kovach was quite looking forward to it. He hadn't blown up a hovercraft in ever so long.

All at once a shadow fell across his screen. He wheeled around in his spinny chair to see who it was, and gulped nervously. "Oh, er, er, sir, commander, I was just, er,"

"You were just *what*, Mr. Kovach?" the Malevolent Med-Student demanded coldly.

"I was just about to open fire on the hovercraft, sir!" Kovach said, leaping to his feet and making a sharp salute. "It refused to identify itself, sir!"

"I see." The Malevolent Med-Student's left eyebrow quirked. "That hovercraft, the one on your screen right now?"

"Yes, sir, that hovercraft exactly, sir!"

"The hovercraft which has *Admiral Zombie Lady* displayed in prominent letters on its side?"

Kovach faltered. "Well, yes..."

"The hovercraft which, by no small coincidence, looks exactly like the one in the memo sent out this morning, which informed you that Admiral Zombie Lady was expected to arrive tonight at 2200 hours? Which, incidentally, is exactly what time it is now?"

The minion began to think he had made a mistake. He fell back with a thump on protocol. "Well, they hadn't identified themselves, sir, and the handbook states in Rule 3.2 that, er,"

"I don't care *what* the rule says! I gave you specific orders, Kovach! That hovercraft is extremely important to my villainous scheme! Without it, I might as well go back to making blueberry muffins laced with a powerful laxative and distributing them at bake sales! I'm not going back, Kovach! I won't!"

"Of course not, sir!" Kovach said, though he wasn't entirely clear what he was agreeing to.

"Exactly!" the Malevolent Med-Student ranted. "Now, you had better stand down the rockets, engage the auto-landing sequence, and get that hovercraft into landing pad B so I can see what's gone amiss, or so help me I will let Susan deal with you. And believe me, you don't want that. She's got all sorts of nasty punishments she's eager to inflict on people who cross her. One of them's got sporks. Rusted pointy sporks. I didn't ask what she wanted to use them for. You don't want to find out, Kovach. You really don't."

"Y-yes sir!" Kovach said, before practically diving to the controls that switched off the rockets and guided the hovercraft in. He had a fear bordering on pure terror of Susan, ever since she'd shown up in Blackacre. He didn't particularly want to know what she wanted the sporks for either.

So the volcano's computer system linked up with the hovercraft, and slowly brought it inside, guiding it gently down onto the landing pad. Catrina, still inside and very much relieved that she hadn't been blown up after all, couldn't help but be impressed. The hanger she'd flown into was brightly lit, none of your dim green or blue lighting that added a villainous flair but which left lots of shadows for intruding heroes to hide it. No, the chamber was lit with bright fluorescent lights, which also made it energy efficient and protected the environment, which was all the rage amongst the villains right then. Susan was old school, of course; she had a kitten-fur jacket with a reversible Dalmatian puppy side, and she just hated the environment, but the Malevolent Med-Student felt one had to keep up with the times.

The cockpit slid open as the hovercraft's systems powered down. This was usually the point where Catrina would've powered up her Sporksaber and leapt out to confront the bad guys, but of course she still had the Control-Flower attached to her head. So she sat there staring blankly at nothing in particular, though inside she was wishing dire things to everyone in her peripheral vision.

The Malevolent Med-Student strode to the parked hovercraft, Susan at his side. He was about to say something pithy and villainous when Susan interrupted in a burst of laughter. "Oh, this is *beautiful!* Catrina! With the

Control-Flower! Ha! My lucky day! Oh man, I have waited whole *scenes* for this!"

"Er, you know her?" the Malevolent Med-Student asked, rather obviously.

"Duh, yeah," Susan said. "She's my nemesis from way back. Keeps stopping me from destroying reality. You know how frustrating that gets? I mean, here I am, going about my business, just trying to live my life and wipe out everybody else's, and can she leave me alone? Nooooooo!"

The Malevolent Med-Student balked. Like most standard villains, he didn't really mean the parts in his speeches where he dramatically proclaimed his desire to destroy the world. Conquer it, sure, force its people to surrender to his whims, yeah, form the world's people into a slave labor army that would build a giant statue of his head in North Dakota, absolutely. But wiping out reality seemed a bit too far for him. Before he could object, though, Susan had already leaned in to look at the Control Flower. "Right, so it's probably keyed to Admiral Zombie Lady's voice, but if I make this little adjustment right here, then maybe...ah-ha! It worked! Okay then! Catrina, I hereby order you to come out of that hovercraft, get out on the pad here, and then I command you to....*riverdance."*

Catrina dutifully unbuckled her seatbelt (all the best hovercrafts had them), climbed out onto the landing pad, dropped her hands to her sides, and began jigging up a storm. "Son of a motherless goat!" the Malevolent Med-Student exclaimed. "It works! I am a genius!"

"I'm sorry," Susan said sweetly. "Who's a genius?"

"Me, naturally! I successfully arranged with Admiral Zombie Lady to bring me the Zombification Dart-Thrower and the Control Flowers, so I could use them as part of my brilliant plan!"

Catrina's shoulder-devil poofed into outraged existence over his shoulder. "Excuse me, *whose* brilliant plan? I think I came up with the Control Flowers bit; *you* were going to use some stupid deathtrap like wild marmosets!"

"And just what is wrong with wild marmosets?" Susan demanded, rather less sweetly.

"Nothing, except it's stupid. And it didn't work, obviously. See Catrina, there, *not* messily devoured?"

"Wild marmosets," the Malevolent Med-Student chortled. "What, the pet stores were all out of alligators?"

"Oh, like your deathtrap was so much better!" Susan snapped. "Giant buzz-saw wheels? Really? That sort of thing went out with the alligators!"

"Right, of course, we don't use silly things like alligators anymore, now we use marmosets!"

Susan fumed. "*That* does it. One more crack about my marmosets and I'm going to send you to Character Hell."

The Malevolent Med-Student had a feeling he wasn't going to win this argument, so he prudently gave up. "Fine. You're right. Marmosets are creative and villainous. You win. May we move on with my evil plan now, the one that doesn't involve destroying reality?"

"After you," Susan said frostily, gesturing to the hovercraft. It was clear she wasn't about to forgive him for insulting her marmoset plan. The Malevolent Med-Student wondered why he had gotten in a relationship with her in the first place. Supervillain relationships never did work out well. On the other hand, she had really cool laser pistols. That was a plus, to be sure.

He popped upon the hovercraft's cargo container. Inside was a completely assembled Zombification Dart-Thrower, complete with an instruction manual. Beside it, piled neatly in a cardboard box, were six white Control-Flowers. The Malevolent Med-Student smiled viciously. "Excellent. Admiral Zombie Lady came through. I wonder where she went, incidentally?"

"Who cares?" Susan said, shrugging. "She was a twip, anyway. Not even named accurately. You wanna test these?"

"I think they've been tested enough," said the Malevolent Med-Student, gesturing to Catrina who was still riverdancing away by the hovercraft's bow. "If we attach them tonight, we can begin the invasion of Edison City by sunrise!"

"Hey now, hold on, I thought we were attacking Tidal!" Susan said. "Make up your mind, will you?"

"I never said anything about Tidal. Edison City is the place of my birth. It is the place that rejected me because I was different from them, the place that became so afraid of me that they denied me my medical degree and threw me out of medical school, the place that cast me out from the spring of academia into the bitter winter of my discontent!"

"You know what this is?" Susan said, holding up two fingers and rubbing them together. "It's the world's tiniest little violin and it's playing the saddest little song just for you. Whiner. I got kicked out of Character Hell, but do you hear me complaining about it? No. Because I got stuff better to do. Now, just to be clear, where are we attacking?

Because you were talking about Tidal earlier. I distinctly remember that."

"We are attacking," the Malevolent Med-Student said, very slowly, in an attempt to control his irritation with his diabolical girlfriend, "Edison City. Tomorrow. At first light. And as the dawn rises over their doomed city, every living soul in it shall know my *revenge!*"

"Yeah, yeah, yeah, I've heard it all before. I'm gonna go take a nap; wake me when the revenge-y stuff starts, will ya? Bye." With that, Susan departed, leaving Catrina still quietly riverdancing in her wake.

"Wake me when the revenge-y stuff starts," the Malevolent Med-Student repeated sourly, once he was sure she was out of earshot. "Yeah, sure. Just you wait, Su. Much more of that, and we're going to have to rethink our relationship." He gathered up the Control-Flowers and started to walk away, then glanced back at Catrina. "You can stop riverdancing now. You'll be picked up later. We have a city to take over, you know!" He gave a dramatic flourish of his white medical lab-coat, and then strode away.

Catrina stood there by the hovercraft, alone. She was moderately relieved to have been allowed to stop riverdancing, but she was furious that she'd been left there like an old umbrella. As time wore on, the fluorescent lights eventually powered down, and the whole landing pad bay went dark. All Catrina could hear was the distant hum of air-conditioning machines, and various muffled clanks that came from other landing bays inside the volcano. She couldn't see for anything. She soon became very, very bored.

At first she tried running through songs she knew, but she didn't know all that many. She knew the Shmirmingard Castle song, her personal theme song, and Susan's theme song, and she recalled them all, every verse. But after that, and one or two folk songs she'd learned from her kingdom's peasantry, her musical repertoire dried up. Almost. Catrina suddenly remembered one other song she had learned, during her first excursion to Character Hell...and she shuddered. Bored as she was, she wasn't desperate enough for "Friday". Not again. Not ever.

She tried composing a poem, taking a cue from her literary friend Ermingard. Catrina wasn't much of a poet, though, and what she eventually came up with was a stirring ode to a blueberry muffin she had eaten recently. At least, she came up with part of a stirring ode; she foundered on a rhyme for muffin, and gave it up in despair. And still nothing happened.

The night wore on, and on, and Catrina began to wonder if she had been forgotten. Maybe the Malevolent Med-Student had changed his mind and decided not to use her in whatever evil scheme she was planning. Catrina tossed that idea aside, though; the Malevolent Med-Student might forget about it, but it was a sure bet that Susan wouldn't. Especially since she seemed to have teamed up with Catrina's shoulder-devil.

That memory sent a sudden ray of hope through Catrina's trapped mind. Her shoulder-angel! Maybe she could get Catrina out of this! She'd gotten Catrina out of scrapes before, hadn't she? But the hope died almost as soon as it had come, as Catrina remembered that she had no idea how to contact her shoulder angel. It just seemed to appear at random moments to offer profound moral advice. Maybe it would show up if Catrina were in dire peril, but then, it hadn't been much help during the Pit O' Marmosets crisis. Catrina resigned herself to the fact that no one was coming for her, angel or otherwise. She was stuck there, alone, until the morning.

That thought wasn't entirely accurate, as it turned out. A few hours before dawn, a small door in the landing pad bay squeaked open, sending a jet of yellow light into the bay and playing across Catrina's face. "Right, come on then!" the Malevolent Med-Student said. "The battle awaits!"

Catrina willed herself not to move forward, but of course she did, marching along after the Malevolent Med-Student as he walked quickly through the vast network of corridors that honeycombed the volcano. Catrina had to admit that the place was impressive. Everywhere she looked she saw black-clad minions marching in good order, weapons ready at their sides. The walls bristled with security cameras, gun emplacements, and trapdoors that could spring closed to halt an enemy in their tracks. Catrina admitted once again that it would be awfully hard launching an assault on this place. Not that she couldn't try; in the wee hours of the morning Catrina had already started working out a plan of attack. If she could only get herself back again, and then get to her Sporksaber...

Then the Malevolent Med-Student went through a last corridor into a huge vaulted chamber, lit with brilliant floodlights, and operatic music playing in the background. Ranks of minions greeted him, standing to attention and making brisk salutes as he passed. They weren't nearly as respectful to Catrina, yelling rude remarks at her as she plodded along in the Malevolent Med-Students' wake.

Catrina pointedly ignored them, which was a lot easier to do since she couldn't say anything anyway. The Malevolent Med-Student soon got through the assembled crowd, and bounded up a small set of metal steps onto a wide platform. At the podium stood Susan, smiling hugely, her twin laser blasters securely holstered at her side. "About time you got here," she said, still smiling. "I almost had to make the usual speech for you. Probably would've done better too."

"And that's why I love you," the Malevolent Med-Student said, not entirely sincerely. "But as much as I would've enjoyed hearing your villain speech, I've been waiting a lot longer for this than you have. Also I wrote mine down on flashcards." He turned and glanced around the hall. "Kovach!" he roared. "Flashcards!"

The minion ran forward, having been relieved of his rocket-monitoring duty specifically to help with the preparation for the Malevolent Med-Student's big speech. He thrust a pack of light blue flashcards into the supervillain's hands. "Here you are, sir!" he said, before scurrying back to take his place in the assembled crowd.

Susan signaled to a waiting collection of musically-inclined minions: the Choir Dire, who struck up an ominous Latin chant as the Malevolent Med-Student strode to the podium, and the spotlights in the assembly hall swung his way. The Choir Dire fell silent on cue. Catrina would've rolled her eyes if she could have; with all this useless pageantry, it was a wonder these supervillains ever got anything else done.

The Malevolent Med-Student paused for a long, dramatic moment. It had been a long time since he'd had the opportunity to deliver a speech, and he needed to make it count. "My dear minions," he began, his voice echoing around the assembly hall. Then he went for his first flashcard. "To do!" the Malevolent Med-Student announced impressively. "Renew membership in the Minion Employees' Union! Buy salt and vinegar chips from the commissary! Make sure I have...clean...socks..."

A faint giggle, quickly suppressed, came from somewhere in the minion crowd. The Malevolent Med-Student shot a terrifying glare at Kovach, who frantically checked his pockets. The unfortunate minion pulled out a second set of flashcards and sheepishly approached the podium, holding them out for his leader. "Er...heh, heh...I think I gave you the wrong-"

"Susan," the Malevolent Med-Student said calmly. "Dispose of him."

Susan stepped forward. "Joelicus Shumacherian!" she said, waving her hands around in an arcane mystical spell. Kovach vanished in a flash of neon pink light.

"Now, would you mind telling everyone here where you've sent our unfortunate ex-minion?"

"Of course," Susan said. "I sent him off to a pocket dimension in Character Hell, where all you lot go when you die. Basically he's trapped for all eternity in a movie theatre that only plays really, really awful films. Films like *Batman and Robin,* or *The Oogieloves and their Big Balloon Adventure.* And those films won't stop playing. They'll go on, and on, and on. And Kovach won't be able to leave. And he'll always have to use the bathroom, but he'll never be able to go. *Forever."*

A shudder of horror ran through the minions. The Malevolent Med-Student nodded. "Thank you. I don't suppose there's any real need to give the speech now. Let's just skip ahead to the main event, shall we? Basically, I'm launching an attack on Edison City in a few hours. But I'm not attacking it myself."

"Wait a sec," Susan interrupted. "I thought you said-"

The Malevolent Med-Student barreled on, completely ignoring his alleged girlfriend. "No, as fun as that would be, that's not quite the revenge I had in mind. Thanks to the Control Flowers provided to me by Admiral Zombie Lady, I have enlisted six of the city's own heroes in our cause. And which heroes did I choose, you may be asking yourselves?" The Malevolent Med-Student's smile grew into a positively feral grin. "Ladies and gentlemen, I give you Edison City's very own nuclear family!"

He gestured dramatically towards a large red curtain at the back of the platform, which swooshed open at his signal. There stood Aaron, Tamsin, the Twins, Sauna, and Caden, each one with a Control Flower attached to their head. The minions, realizing what he had done, broke into wave after wave of applause.

"You all know their abilities!" the Malevolent Med-Student said, forgetting that many of the minions didn't know that, since none of the kids were licensed to use their powers in public except for Aaron, and he only had a permit. "You know what they can do, what havoc they can unleash upon Edison City! And that's not all! When they go into battle against the city's remaining heroes, they won't be led by me. Oh, no. They will be led by someone who the city already thinks is set against them! Minions, I give you...*Zombie Catrina!*"

The applause was more muted this time, since very few of the minions even knew who Catrina was, let alone

Zombie Catrina. But then Susan produced Catrina's own red Sporksaber, which she had stolen from the Edison City jail during the confusion of the attack on it. She tossed it to Catrina, who caught it upon her command and swiftly ignited it. The red blade, part curve and part gleaming point, lit Catrina's face with an eerie glow, and the minions' applause grew louder. It grew into a thunderous roar as the Twins cloned themselves out to line the platform, as Tamsin shifted into her Frisbee form and shot around the assembly hall, as Sauna melted the podium into slag. "To the hovercrafts!" the Malevolent Med-Student boomed. "The liberation of Edison City begins now!"

Of course that was all for show. Launching an invasion of anywhere is a massive undertaking that requires a good deal of organization and logistics. The Malevolent Med-Student and Susan managed to get Catrina and her small army of zombified superheroes assigned to the right hovercrafts, but then they had to coordinate launch times and flight paths, make sure the hovercrafts were fully fueled, check weather maps for storms in their way, and take care of half a dozen other things that really should have been planned for in advance. The Malevolent Med-Student's goal of attacking Edison City at dawn turned out to be wildly optimistic. Catrina and her flotilla of attack hovercraft didn't set off from Blackacre until ten in the morning, which meant they wouldn't even arrive at Edison City until late in the afternoon, at best. But they would arrive, and Susan looked very much forward to watching the battle unfold on the huge screens in Blackacre's command center. She couldn't wait to see Zombie Catrina in action, even if the zombie label was slightly inaccurate.

Chapter Eleven

Tasha and Meg had gone back to Edison City, each one trying to deal as best they could with what had happened. Tasha didn't have a job to bury herself in; when she wasn't doing superhero work she had been a typical stay-at-home mom. But now she had no home to stay in. So she went out on patrol, circling through the city and looking for people to save and bad guys to pummel. But even then Super Soccer Mom felt like she was operating on autopilot. She couldn't let herself think about her family, about Justin or the kids. So she didn't. She concentrated on patrolling. Winston floated beside her; the soccer ball seemed as distressed as she was, in the limited intelligence it had.

Meg Atomic hadn't taken her mom's approach; instead she had retreated into her apartment and locked the door behind her. She sat dismally on her bed, knees drawn up, staring out of the window, trying to make sense of it all. Her formidable predictive powers had failed her. She hadn't guessed that Drew would go that bad, or that her family would be wiped out. She hadn't seen it coming at all. And since she hadn't, she didn't know if she could ever trust herself again. Worse, Drew had lied to her, had used her, had manipulated her parents into wrecking their marriage, and she hadn't figured it out until it was too late. She couldn't forgive herself for that. So she sat there, alone, waiting for something to change.

Then her cell phone rang. Meg ignored it. She guessed it might be her mother; Tasha would be the most logical one to call her, but Meg didn't particularly want to talk to anyone right now. She pulled her cellphone from her pocket and took out the battery, then flung them both aside. She didn't have a landline, so now no one would be calling her. Meg had forgotten, though, that her cell phone wasn't her only communications device. She had a radio specially keyed to a certain frequency, like the weather radios that go off whenever there is a severe thunderstorm warning. Only this radio wasn't about the weather. This radio went off whenever there was a major supervillain crisis that required every hero in the city to suit up. It hadn't gone off for months. Now, as she turned back to the window, its loud air-horn siren filled her apartment. Meg hit the talk button more out of morbid curiosity than anything else. Surely, whatever crisis it was, they could handle it without her. She would probably muck it up anyway. She-what was this?

"Repeating, this is a citywide crisis alert. Jill Polarity and Catrina have been sighted in the North End. Jill Polarity has been confirmed as carrying the Kaboominator. They appear reinforced by four supervillains, possibly minors, and a small army of child-sized clones. All available superheroes please respond. Repeating, this is a citywide crisis..."

But Meg was already running for the door. She knew of only two people in the city who could clone themselves. If the Twins had survived, that meant maybe the others had. Whatever they were doing with Catrina and Jill Polarity, she had to get there. She ran out into the street, and glanced around for her motorcycle (a standard mode of transportation for younger superheroes who hadn't scraped up the money to buy a car yet). Then Super Soccer Mom swooped in, holding on to Winston. "You heard?" she said.

"Yeah," Meg replied. "You think it's them?"

"I don't know. They wouldn't have gone bad, not unless..."

Meg's eyes flamed in yellow-white fury. "Not unless Drew did something to them."

No more needed to be said. They tore off, heading for the North End, Meg on her bike and Winston carrying Tasha with its flight attachment. Lucy radioed in that she would meet them there as soon as she could; unfortunately she was some ways across the city, and the other members of the Phenomenal Four were out of town. Trina was on vacation with her daughter in Florida, and Natalie was working in Europe. Tasha really wished Natalia hadn't been away; being invulnerable could be really useful right now.

Marsha had gone to the Edison City Public Library to do some quiet reading. She was pretty sure she'd have the time to do this without getting interrupted, even if she did live in a superhero town. After all, what kind of supervillain would attack a library? Maybe the really bad ones, the ones who did it for the sheer joy of being evil and who meant what they said about destroying the world, but for the most part Edison's supervillains weren't that intense. They adhered to standards, to conventions. In Edison City, one of those conventions was that the library was off-limits.

So Marsha was as surprised as anyone when a red energy blade sliced through the automatic doors at the front of the library, followed by a magenta-tinged Volvo that smashed through the doors and demolished the circulation desk, sending the librarians screaming for cover. "Hey!" Marsha protested. "This is the library! You're not supposed to attack here!"

Zombie Catrina stalked through the wreckage of the doorway, casually flicking her Sporksaber right through a set of Twilight volumes and setting them ablaze. She didn't say anything, but Jill Polarity did. Jill staggered through the smoke behind her, lugging the Kaboominator. "This *was* the library," she puffed (Jill wasn't the most in-shape of supervillains; she'd thought seriously about going on a diet). "Now, it's our headquarters. Clones!" she yelled back at Jamie and Jeremy. "Secure the building!"

Jamie and Jeremy, and their small army of duplicates, fanned out across the New Books section and marched up the stairs to the Children's and Young Adults section in their own recreation of the famous Odessa Steps sequence from the *Battleship Potemkin* movie. As they were zombified two-year-olds and not Russian soldiers, and as the steps were only one short flight up, the effect wasn't quite as dramatic.

Jill set up the Kaboominator amidst what was left of the circulation desk. "Now, if anyone comes, we'll blast them out of the sky!"

"Hey..." Candystriper said, having just arrived. She'd awakened from her nap only recently, heard about the crisis at the library, and decided she should probably be over there. "Whoa. Trippy. By the way, you really really don't want to fire that thing. Big explosion, you know?"

Jill Polarity rolled her magenta eyes. "That's kinda the point."

"No, no, see, there's too much recoil. Marcie explained it all. The Kaboominator isn't, like, balanced properly, so when you set it off the recoil kicks you back and it hurts. A lot. Trust me, I know; my head's killing me right now. Colon left-parenthesis."

"Colon what?" Jill asked, in astonishment. "Did you just try to use an emoticon in actual dialogue?"

But Candystriper had lost interest in the conversation, having gotten distracted by the lovely bonfire consuming the Twilight series. "Ooh, should I add in more?" she pleaded.

Jill was beginning to wish the Malevolent Med-Student, or Susan (whoever she was) had come along instead of radioing ahead to have her take charge. "No. We're not burning any more books."

She apparently should've mentioned that to Sauna, who had just walked in and promptly ignited a rack of large-print mysteries, as heat energy spilled uncontrollably from her like a burst fire hydrant. Jill sighed. "You know what? Forget this. Sauna, you and Tamsin go back outside. You'll be the first line of defense. Catrina, Aaron, Caden, you stay in here; you're second line. If they get in and start attacking, Aaron you neutralize their powers, and Zombie Catrina, you hit 'em with the Sporksaber. Caden, well, you're useless, 'cause all you do is not sleep, so you handle the Kaboominator. Fire it if it looks like everyone else is losing. Jamie, Jeremy, you keep an eye on the place, make sure no one's sneaking in from behind."

"So, what're you going to do?" Candystriper asked in a rare moment of clear thinking.

"I'm leaving. I did my bit, I told you guys what to do. I don't want revenge on Edison City; that's the Malevolent Med-Student's bit. He isn't paying me nearly enough for this." With that, Jill Polarity slipped out an emergency door and ran off into the evening. She had abruptly decided that being in the major supervillain leagues was too much hassle. Jill figured that no one would really notice that she had left, and after all she hadn't done too much damage, and....she paused suddenly, halfway down an alleyway, and her mouth went dry with fear. "Um. Oh. It's you. Heh. You're back. Um. Look, I just want to say, it wasn't my idea and I'm really sorry-"

She was about to be a whole lot more sorry. She figured that out as she arced through the air, seconds before she landed hard against a tree. Jill Polarity wouldn't be figuring much else out for a long while.

Meanwhile, back at the library, Tasha and Meg had just rounded the street corner and arrived at the front steps. "Sauna!" Tasha exclaimed, sudden tears starting to her eyes. "Thank heaven it's you, I-"

But Sauna, her face unmoving, turned and extended her hand towards her mother, and a wave of heat smacked into Super Soccer Mom like a solid fist, knocking her backward and scorching her uniform badly. A few flames started up, but Winston swooped in and opened up with a flame-retardant jet. Then Winston turned the jet towards Sauna, who blasted it with all the heat she could muster, and the duel was on.

Tasha saw the white flower on Sauna's head, and realized instantly what it meant; she had fought Admiral Zombie Lady before. Meg spotted it too. All at once everything clicked together in her head, and she Saw It All. Before she could explain to her mother, though, a purple Frisbee thwacked against her head. "Ow! Tamsin, stop that....oh, never mind. You wouldn't listen even if you weren't zombified."

Meg would've been more torn-up about her younger sister being under the supervillain's control, but the thing of it was, she knew Tamsin almost better than anyone, and she knew particularly that her sister in Frisbee form was nigh-invulnerable. As in, very very close to invulnerable, but not quite. So when she unleashed a small atomic blast, she knew how to make it just powerful enough to send Tamsin flipping away into the sky, but not so powerful that it wouldn't hurt her sister or even force her to shift back to human form. Tamsin wouldn't be back for several minutes. That would give her time to deal with Sauna.

But in that moment Meg hesitated. Could she trust her calculations? She'd been wrong about Drew, hadn't she? Suppose she was wrong about this? Suppose she used the wrong amount of atomic force? Meg saw Tamsin hurtling towards her again, at a speed which means Tamsin was coming in for the kill, or at least a really bad concussion. Meg didn't particularly want either. She took a quick breath, raised her hand, and fired an atomic power burst that sent the purple Frisbee flipping backwards. It turned out she had miscalculated, just slightly. Tamsin didn't go shooting off into the sky. No, instead she flipped right into Sauna, who had just ducked around Winston and been about to torch her own mother. Sauna hadn't seen the Frisbee coming, and crumpled unconscious to the ground, the heat dying around her. Tamsin circled around and started for Meg again, but Meg fired again, and this time she got the angle right. Tamsin bounced away into the stratosphere.

Tasha sighed, watching her Frisbee daughter go. She was slightly relieved. Winston had all sorts of countermeasures in case any of her children went rogue, just like the sound pulse that jammed the Twins' cloning abilities. So she could have simply given a thought and Winston would've zapped Sauna with a cryogenic ray that would've frozen her solid. But somehow, Tasha couldn't quite bring herself to do it. It wasn't Sauna's fault, for heaven's sake; it was the Control Flower. This wasn't like when she'd had to secure Tamsin in a ray shield because she kept bonking little Tyler on the head as a Frisbee in first grade. This was different. So that was why she was grateful that Meg's miscalculation had taken care of things. The trouble was, she was going to have to do it again. She still had four children under Admiral Zombie Lady's control, not to mention Jill Polarity and Catrina and the Kaboominator to worry about.

"You okay, Mom?" Meg asked.

Tasha nodded, staring down at the unconscious Sauna and the white flower at her head. "I wish I knew how to get rid of this thing. The old-model Control Flowers I heard one could just pull out, but these new ones are wired right into the nervous system. We'd need a medical person for this."

"Right," Meg agreed. "In the meantime, the rest of them will be inside. I suppose we could just go straight in...."

Meg's eyes narrowed as she considered, and Tasha could practically hear the wheels going in her daughter's brain. She had always admired that about Meg, even when it got awkward during high school when Meg demonstrated conclusively that she really was smarter than her mother, and could provide a full academic treatise on why she should be allowed to go with Ryan to the spring formal and stay out past her bedtime. Tasha had been forced to play the "because I'm your mother and I said so" card more than the usual.

"No," Meg decided at last. "If we go straight in they could just use the Kaboominator against us and end it right there. Of course they could hold back their superweapon and not use it until the last resort, but that would be illogical. If they're smart they'll use the Kaboominator as soon as they can and save the expense of fighting."

"This is exactly why I wanted Natalie for this," Tasha said unhappily. "She survived a nuclear explosion once, she would be great for the Kaboominator."

Meg smiled. "And I can *make* nuclear explosions. So I should go in direct and draw their fire. You should circle around behind and go in through the back. There's a 65 percent chance you would be able to take at least some of them by surprise."

"65%?" Tasha inquired. "Are you certain you can't give me 70? Maybe 80, even?"

Her daughter shrugged. "I already factored in Winston. There's nothing else I can think off that would increase the odds. If you waited for Lucy, maybe..."

"No, we don't have time. We've got to take down the Kaboominator now. I'll see you inside, Meg." They hugged fiercely; Tasha wasn't terribly worried that she was going to lose Meg, but one never knew anymore. She hadn't thought she would ever lose her captain. Her eyes misty with the memory, she jogged away around the side of the library, Winston floating along at her side.

Zombie Catrina hadn't moved from her spot near the demolished circulation desk, her Sporksaber humming in her hand. Aaron stood next to her, waiting for someone to attack so he could flip their superpowers against them. Caden manned the Kaboominator, aiming it right at the main entrance of the library. They seemed ready for a whole army of superheroes to come charging inside. Candystriper, meanwhile, had picked up a nature magazine about platypuses and become engrossed in it. She had lost interest in the battle entirely, which was understandable since she'd been given nothing to do. She thought she had seen something in her peripheral vision, a flash that vaguely reminded her of someone she'd seen before, but Candystriper petulantly decided that if no one wanted her help, then they wouldn't get her help. So there.

At any rate, Zombie Catrina and her companions had braced themselves for a full-scale onslaught. What they had not prepared for was Meg, by herself, picking her way gingerly through the wreck of the front entrance. "Hey," Meg said, waving. "I will attack momentarily. I just need to get past this beam. Be with you in a tick."

None of the three quite knew what to do. Caden had been ordered not to fire the Kaboominator until it looked like everyone else was losing; so far the battle hadn't even started. Aaron and Zombie Catrina had been told not to start in until the superheroes attacked, but Meg hadn't actually attacked yet. So, since they hadn't been ordered to take initiative, they just stood around like idiots and waited.

Meg could've simply blown the wreckage out of her way, naturally, but she had chosen the hard route because she had wanted to see what they would do. It looked like the Control Flowers hadn't given her siblings very much latitude. Then she blinked. Catrina wore a Control Flower too. All this time everyone had thought Catrina was working for the bad guys. But if she were, why would they have needed to stick a Control Flower on her? Meg Saw It All, again. She also decided that she'd had enough of clambering through wreckage; a simple burp of power sliced the remaining beam out of the way, and she stepped fully into the library. "So, then," she said, "who's first?"

That sounded like a challenge to Zombie Catrina, and a challenge meant attack, and that meant she could go. She started forward, Sporksaber held high, with the not unreasonable goal that she would cut Meg's arm off. As she did, Aaron stepped towards his sister as well, intent on reversing her superpowers. He hadn't done this to Meg before, but he expected either that her explosions would reverberate back on herself and send her flying, or maybe that her immunity from nuclear radiation would break down and she'd fall over and throw up. To his dull zombified astonishment, nothing happened. Meg calmly power-blasted Zombie Catrina halfway across the library, right smack into the audiobook shelf.

"I imagine you do not understand why your power did not work on me," she said. She then launched into a complicated explanation about genetics and radiation and how his power was related to radioactivity in some complicated way and her powers involved radioactivity absorption in an even more complicated way. It was really a mercy when Zombie Catrina came running back and tried to cut off her arm again. Meg swatted her away with another power blast, or at least she tried to, because this time Zombie Catrina deflected the shot with her Sporksaber, causing a reverberating shock that sent both Meg and Aaron tumbling backward. Meg regained herself, took the opportunity to make sure Aaron was unconscious and then quickly power-blasted him into staying that way, and then tried another attack on Zombie Catrina, who deflected as easily as before. Catrina then started slowly advancing towards her, Sporksaber ready to block her power blasts, and Meg decided this would be a very good time for her mother to intervene.

Super Soccer Mom had, meanwhile, gone around back to the library's service entrance. Winston's infrared scanner informed her that five clones stood waiting on the other side of the door, ready to pounce on whoever tried to come in. Tasha wasn't entirely sure what they were supposed to do then; the Twins' only ability was cloning themselves. They didn't have super strength or speed or anything. Maybe if a whole bunch of them ganged up on her they might pose a threat. Five, not so much. On the other hand, Tasha wasn't about to take chances. She glanced around, looking for something she remembered from previous trips to the library, in happier times when her family wasn't all zombified and gross. There, in a corner, she saw a small speaker. She knew that was connected to the library's public address system. Why they had a speaker outside was a question Tasha hadn't the slightest clue how to answer. It wasn't like they were a restaurant where people had to stand outside to wait to get in. Super Soccer Mom couldn't remember a time she had needed to wait in line to get into the library. That was a little sad, come to think of it, and spoke volumes about the state of education in the country. Tasha decided that she would bring this up in the next PTA meeting. In the meantime, she had more pressing concerns on her mind, like how to deal with her zombie two-year-olds who had taken over the library.

She thought a quick command at Winston, who picked up on her idea and ran with it. The soccer ball soared up to the speaker and busily hacked its way inside. Within moments Winston had linked its own computer system to the public address system of the library, and then promptly broadcast the extremely high frequency that jammed the Twins' cloning abilities. The five clones on the other side of the door disappeared. "Nice work, Winston," Tasha said. She pulled the door open and headed inside. Winston followed her, having left a remote link to the public address system so that he could keep on jamming the Twins.

Super Soccer Mom made her way as stealthily as she could through the corridors of the library, which wasn't all that hard to do since she'd been used to being quiet inside the library anyway. She heard explosions in the distance, and guessed that Meg had gone into battle. Tasha quickened her pace, knowing she had to help and soon. Unfortunately, when she rounded the corner of the Mystery section she came face to face with Candystriper, who had lost interest in the platypus magazine and gone in search of something more fun.

Tasha was in no mood to deal with the scatterbrained minion. She glanced towards Winston, starting to order the soccer ball to knock Candystriper out so she could go on. But Candystriper, though she had problems with distraction at times and took advice from a hallucination of a tiny blue manatee named Marcie, was a dangerous minion to underestimate. She had learned a few things from the Malevolent Med-Student. Like, say, the sudden flying kick that slammed against Tasha's solar plexus and knocked the wind right out of her, or the rapid blow that sent Super Soccer Mom spiraling off into unconsciousness. Tasha vaguely noticed, just before she passed out, that Winston had finally deployed its electric stunner and zapped Candystriper, a few seconds too late. *Oh well...* Tasha thought dizzily, as blackness overtook her. *I tried....*

Meg didn't know that her mom wasn't coming. She tried to fend off Catrina, but every atomic power-blast she fired got blasted right back at her by the crackling energy of the Sporksaber blade. Meg wondered in curious desperation what that thing was made of. She didn't recognize it at all. Pity, to be defeated by something she didn't understand.

She tried again and again, but Zombie Catrina kept on coming, closer and closer with every precise step. Meg had one weapon left in her arsenal; she could unleash a flood of radiation that would stagger Zombie Catrina physically, weakening her enough for Meg to come in and knock her out. But Meg had never liked the radiation assault; it was too uncontrollable. She couldn't focus it like she could her atomic power-blasts, which meant that it wouldn't be just Catrina, it would be Aaron, and Caden over by the Kaboominator, and probably everyone in the library, which included the Twins, not to mention her mom. Meg swiftly calculated the probable futures of her unleashing the radiation wave, and balanced them against the probable futures of her *not* doing it, and as she was working all that out Catrina moved in a sudden blur and snap-kicked Meg into the rack of romance paperbacks.

When she opened her eyes again, Zombie Catrina stood over her, Sporksaber raised high. Meg had a sudden dazed uncomfortableness as she realized that the blade wasn't aimed at her arm this time. No, Zombie Catrina was going for the death blow. The worse of it was, in her zombified state she wasn't even going to deliver some sort of pithy remark. Meg missed that; it was tradition for the villains to say things just before they killed the hero. She had often imagined what would be said about her. Probably some horrible pun about sub-atomics. She would never know now.

Zombie Catrina's blade started to descend, and Meg closed her eyes, not wanting to see it as it swept down towards her neck. Then, in the distance, she heard a sudden thunderclap that sounded oddly familiar. Meg's eyes flew open in time to see a red-white blur cannon into Zombie Catrina, sending her careening straight through a plate-glass window out of the library. Meg's mouth dropped open in disbelief. *"Dad?"*

Captain Happily Married stood tall and proud amidst the scattered romance paperbacks, his boots planted uncaringly on the pictures of the ridiculously posed and unseasonably clad cover people, his white cape unfurled dramatically in the sudden wind. "Looks like she's not going to find a pot of gold at the end of her reading rainbow; it seems what she found instead was the mighty and still married fist of justice!"

Meg laughed and cried all at once, making an odd hiccupy-sobbing noise and scrambling for a tissue. No one ever carried tissues in superhero fights; she needed to make a note of this. Then she looked behind him. "Dad, look out!"

But the captain was already moving, just as Caden reached for the big red button that fired up the Kaboominator. He seized the weapon from his son's grasp and then shot straight upwards, blasting through the library ceiling and into the sky. The captain pressed the red button that activated the device, and gave it a second press that engaged its self-destruct option (he had read the manual on it some years ago when it had been invented; it paid to read the literature on these things). Then Captain Happily Married drew back his mighty arm, preparing to hurl the Kaboominator into space where it would explode harmlessly and never be used by anyone ever again. But at that moment Tamsin came hurtling back and struck the Kaboominator from his hand.

The fearsome weapon tumbled downwards and landed right in Zombie Catrina's arms. She had just come upright again after hitting the outside parking lot and bouncing one or two times, landing against an old Bookmobile. Zombie Catrina's orders were still fairly clear; she was supposed to attack and destroy the superheroes. So, rather than tossing the unfamiliar weapon away and running for her life, she ignored the increasingly rapid warning beep it was making and aimed the Kaboominator in the direction of the library. Inside Catrina was practically screaming at her zombified self. "Oh *come on!* I am *not* going to get killed *again* because of some *stupid* self-destructing-"

The Kaboominator lived up to its impressive name. When it went off, it made a very big kaboom indeed. Fortunately, the nearby area had been entirely evacuated of civilians, and Catrina had been thrown into a very wide parking lot. So although the Kaboominator turned the very wide parking lot into a very wide crater, and caused some structural damage to the library, it didn't hurt anyone or cause any major distress. Except for Catrina, of course; she got vaporized in a blink of an eye. But Captain Happily Married was still working under the assumption that she was a supervillain, and he'd seen lots of supervillains get hoisted by their own brightly colored petards in often violent ways, so he wasn't too broken up about it. "Well, looks like that finishes everything off!" he said. "Now, I'd say we have a little field trip we need to make out west. I'd like to have a few words with your ex-boyfriend!"

"So would I," Meg said grimly. "So would I." She was about to mention to the captain her suspicion that maybe Catrina hadn't been one of the bad guys, but at that moment Tasha came limping out of the library, having been woken up by the earth-shattering rumble of the Kaboominator.

"Justin?" she breathed. "*Justin!*" She threw herself forward into his arms, and they shared a very sentimental moment. Winston decorously turned its sensors to examining the Control Flower in Sauna's head, scanning through its memory banks to see if it could find a way to extract the flower without hurting her. Meg walked over to the crater and stared at the spot where Catrina had once been. "I am sorry we could not save you," she said aloud, hoping Catrina, wherever she was, could somehow understand. Then she walked back to rejoin her parents. It looked like their marriage hadn't got wrecked after all. So once again Edison City had been saved. She hoped it would stay saved for a good long while.

Chapter Twelve

Susan swore violently, using words that would've made the entire United States Navy turn red with embarrassment. She had watched the battle on the screens of Blackacre's command center. It hadn't always been the best picture; the Malevolent Med-Student's minion-techies had hacked into security cameras and satellite imaging, and so sometimes the screen was fuzzy and indistinct. But Susan could make out well enough what had happened, especially when she saw the supersonic blur that could only mean one person. Captain Happily Married had returned; her idiot boyfriend and his idiotic padamantium bomb had failed to kill him. Maybe it was for some stupid sentimental reason like the Captain realizing that he did love Tasha after all and he didn't want to break up with her, and knowing from the look in her eyes that she felt the same way, and so their marriage and his powers had been mystically restored just in the nick of time. Or maybe his powers had only been temporarily gone to begin with, since he hadn't actually divorced Tasha yet. Or maybe the author had just randomly decided to give him his powers back as a way to move the story along. Susan didn't know, and she didn't care, but she really, *really* hated losing.

The ex-mistress of all Character Hell had just managed to get control of herself and start calming down when she saw the white bloom of heat that meant the Kaboominator had blown up. The screen also showed one less life sign, which meant that the Kaboominator had taken Catrina with it. "*What!*" Susan shrieked. "*I* was going to kill her! Me! I wanted that for myself! But do I ever get to kill her? No! I don't! This is so stupid! I hate this! It's unfair! It's not right! It-"

"Do you ever shut up?" the Malevolent Med-Student interjected. He wasn't in the best of moods himself. His wonderful plan had fallen apart again. He was beginning to think he should have gone along to supervise.

"Excuse me?" Susan said, her voice low and dangerous. "*Excuse me?* You told me to shut up. *You* told *me* to shut up. Do you have any idea who I am?"

"Yeah, yeah, yeah," the Malevolent Med-Student said. "You're the ex-mistress of all Character Hell. You've said that. Often."

"Ex," Susan snarled. "Always the ex. Well, I think that's gotta change. I swear, that is gonna *change.*" She put her fingers to her lips and gave a piercing whistle. Catrina's shoulder-devil poofed tremulously into existence; it was about as upset at the failure of their plans as the Malevolent Med-Student was. "Time to leave, bucko," Susan snapped at it. "I have had just about *enough* of this *stupid* story."

"But..." the Malevolent Med-Student said, entirely nonplussed. "But you can't just leave! They're probably going to come back here and attack Blackacre; you've got to help me!"

"Yeah? Talk to the hand," Susan retorted. "Because the face ain't listening."

The Malevolent Med-Student chortled. "Su, the 1990s just called. They want their slang insult back."

"Well, when you give it back to them, make sure to give back that joke as well, because I haven't heard that *since* the 1990s! Shoulder devil?" she said, rounding upon the terrified tiny creature. "We're leaving. *Now.*"

"Okay okay okay!" squeaked the little incarnation of evil. It waved its pitchfork around dramatically, and both Susan and it disappeared, never again to appear in the story.

The Malevolent Med-Student looked around. The minion techies still in the command center stared uncomprehendingly back at him. The Malevolent Med-Student felt the time was right to say something heroic, but he hadn't a clue what. Kovach had been a decent speechwriter, now that he came to think of it. He almost wished Susan hadn't packed the minion off to a pocket dimension in Character Hell. Still, he supposed he had to say something.

"Well," he began unconvincingly. "Well. My fellow minions. We're in a bit of a jam, it seems, but don't worry, because deep down inside, I know we're all going to stick together, just like peanut butter. The peanut butter of evil! And when you add peanut butter to jam and stick them in between two slices of bread, what do you get?"

"Um..." a minion volunteered. "A peanut-butter and jelly sandwich?"

"I don't think I heard you. Say that again!"

"A peanut butter and jelly sandwich," the minion said, a little louder.

"Again!"

"A peanut butter and jelly sandwich!"

"One more time!"

"A PEANUT BUTTER AND JELLY SANDWICH!" the minion roared, leaping up on a table, having been carried away with the excitement.

"Exactly!" the Malevolent Med-Student thundered. "And not just any peanut butter and jelly sandwich, no, this is the peanut butter and jelly sandwich of victory! And we're going to eat that sandwich! And then we're going to eat the Oreo cookies of the despair of our enemies, dunking them in the milk of their humiliation!"

The minions in the command cheered wildly. Their cheers were suddenly cut short by the blaring of alarm klaxons. *Warning,* Blackacre's computer informed them in its usual calm monotone. *Intruder alert. Superheroes are now approaching the perimeter, sandwich metaphors notwithstanding.*

The Malevolent Med-Student made a mental note to reprogram that computer; it had taken a decidedly snotty turn ever since he'd caught Susan tinkering with it the other day. "Battle stations!" he roared, and the minions all scurried off to their posts. Rockets soon filled the sky, lighting it up with blinding flashes. The Malevolent Med-Student watched the screens closely, hoping to see the superheroic figures heading for his island tumbling out of the sky. No such luck. Not one of the rockets seemed to have an impact. Or, to be more accurate, some of them were impacting, but they were impacting on Captain Happily Married, who apparently found their explosive blasts to be mildly irritating at the most. Meanwhile, the rockets that didn't smack up against the nigh-invulnerable captain were being blasted into bits by Meg Atomic, or shot out of the sky by laser bolts from Winston, or exploding soccer balls hurled by Super Soccer Mom.

The Malevolent Med-Student knew good and well that if his rockets weren't going to stop them, then the gun emplacements that honeycombed the island wouldn't do much good either. Bullets would just bounce harmlessly off the captain, and Winston would only take a second to throw up a ray shield that would protect Super Soccer Mom and Tasha. "So much for that," the Malevolent Med-

Student said. "Time to find another secret villain lair." He had an escape pod, of course, hidden near the volcano's peak. He'd only built one; the Malevolent Med-Student didn't much care whether his loyal minions escaped or not. To that end, he hadn't quite gotten around to telling them yet about the self-destruct sequence he had built into the lair. True, self-destruct sequences hadn't worked out so well for him thus far (see: the Kaboominator), but this time he was sure it would work. All he had to do was key it in and make his getaway, and Captain Happily Married would be blown to smithereens!

"It's perfect!" the Malevolent Med-Student shouted. "It's absolutely brilliant!" What he said next was completely inexcusable. He had made that mistake many times before, but he had never learned. He should've known he was tempting fate. He should've known that he ought to have kept his mouth shut, started the self-destruct sequence, and then made his getaway posthaste instead of ranting on about it. But in his heart of hearts, the Malevolent Med-Student was a supervillain, plain and simple. And so it was almost inevitable that he would give a dramatic flourish to his white medical labcoat, turn to face his awed minions, and declaim in a stirring voice, "I am *invincible!*"

The minion techies groaned, and one or two of them actually facepalmed. This wasn't their first tour of duty; they knew full well what those words usually meant. The Malevolent Med-Student was completely oblivious, though, which was why he was completely surprised when Captain Happily Married smashed through the side of Blackacre, tore straight through its steel and rock corridors, and burst through the command center's screens. "You there!" he boomed at the terrified Malevolent Med-Student. "The Hippocratic oath says first do no harm, but I think your case qualifies for an exception!"

"Look, it wasn't my idea, it was all Susan and the shoulder-devil!" the Malevolent Med-Student attempted to explain. "I'll surrender now, okay, and I'll go quietly off to the Tesla Asylum, just don't hurt me, okay?"

"Of course not," Captain Happily Married said, in righteous indignation. "I'm the sworn defender of Edison City, fighting for justice, liberty, and matrimony! I would never dream of attacking an unarmed and defenseless supervillain who has just surrendered to me."

The Malevolent Med-Student breathed a sigh of relief. "That's good to know. I didn't think you wouldn't."

"Right," the captain said, stepping back from the hole he'd blasted through the computer screens. "Which is why I'm going to let you have a word with my daughter."

"Your...oh no."

"Hey," Meg said, yellow flames dancing in her eyes.

"Also," Captain Happily Married continued, smiling gleefully. "My wife would like to join the conversation. I think she and Meg wanted to have a bonding moment."

"Yes," Tasha said, kicking an explosive soccer ball idly about. "Mainly where our fists bond with your face."

"Ah, heh-heh," the Malevolent Med-Student said. "What I said back at the wedding, I didn't really...I broke up with Susan, you know. You did know that, right?"

"How sad," Meg said, not sounding the least bit sorry for him. "'Tis better to have loved and lost, then never loved at all. Actually, it's not, really. Ask me how I know, *Drew*. Go on. *Ask.*"

The Malevolent Med-Student had a sneaking suspicion that she didn't really want him to ask. He was right.

The minion technicians didn't put up a fight to speak of; having seen their leader bounced around the command center like a Ping-pong ball, they wisely decided not to incur Meg's wrath, or Tasha's for that matter. Upon the captain's instructions they evacuated the volcano peacefully and in good order. It turned out that they still had a good fleet of hovercrafts stored away; the minions piled into them and sailed away from Blackacre, watched over by Captain Happily Married flying vigilantly above them. Tasha hacked her way into the command center's control systems and tripped the self-destruct sequence; then she and Meg high-tailed it out of there. They took the Malevolent Med-Student with them. Meg had momentarily considered leaving him behind, but then came to the happy conclusion that death was just too good for him. And so they all flew, or sailed, or powered along by soccer ball, into the east, heading home towards Edison City, as Blackacre merrily blew itself to ash and rubble behind them. The world had been saved once again. So, fortunately, had Captain Happily Married and Tasha's marriage.

Meanwhile, in another world, the barista of the little coffee shop attached to the bookstore where this tale all began was slowly wiping off a table, listening to her iPod and looking very much forward to the end of her shift. All at once there was a flash of golden light, and a black-haired girl materialized in front of her. "Wha!" the barista squeaked, dropping her cleaning cloth in shock.

"Oh," Catrina said. "I'm back. Well. I guess when I got killed in the story, I didn't actually get killed in the real world. How fortunate."

"You...you...you..." the poor barista stuttered. Her reaction was perfectly understandable; she'd had a stressful day, and she was unprepared to see people popping out of thin air like a reverse Rapture. Then she was even more surprised and bewildered when a tiny glowing figure with a tinier halo materialized on Catrina's shoulder.

"Actually," the shoulder angel said, "you didn't get killed in the story. I pulled you out of it in the nick of time. If you'd died there you would've died for real, and I don't think you want that."

"Well, no..." Catrina had to admit. "But you couldn't maybe have done something about the zombie bit?"

"No, I wanted that to be a lesson to you," the shoulder angel replied archly.

"Oh, dear, this is where we get to the moral, isn't it."

From the coffee-shop's overhead speakers came playing the soft sounds of a *Full House* clarinet. "Yes, in fact this is where we get to the moral," the little angel said. "I want you to tell me what you learned from this whole experience."

"I learned that I can communicate with wild marmosets. I have no idea how they'll be useful, but I'm sure it will be eventually."

"Catrina..." said the shoulder-angel warningly.

"Fine," Catrina said, rolling her eyes. "I learned that I shouldn't interfere with someone else's story, that I should let them have their adventure even if I think their decisions are stupid, because otherwise they'll never learn and develop as characters."

"Exactly," the shoulder-angel said. "I also hope you learned that you shouldn't go rushing around waving your Sporksaber and attacking everyone. Maybe you could try a little peaceful diplomacy once in a while. Blessed are the peacemakers, you know."

"So I've heard," Catrina said. "And believe me, I'll be sure to take that to heart." At that moment they heard a crash from outside. Running to the window, Catrina saw a familiar-looking brown-haired girl yelling rude things at a mailman, in whose mail truck she had apparently just materialized. Catrina's slow half-smile spread over her face. "If you'll excuse me," she said, "I'm going to go outside and try some peaceful diplomacy with Susan. I owe that to her after all that riverdancing she had me do. I think we might even have some constructive dialogue and come to mutual understanding. And, failing that..."

She ignited her Sporksaber. Crimson energy blazed in the coffee shop. Catrina's theme song started up on cue. For once, Catrina actually joined in. The other coffee shop patrons did as well; they'd seen impromptu musicals before and they were more than happy to help out. "Everybody!" Catrina said. "I'm Catrina, I am a princess, I don't kill wabbits, that's not what I do! I'm Catrina, this is my theme song, I don't like Susan, neither should you!" Catrina fired off a last salute to the cheering coffee shop patrons, made an apologetic smile at the completely bewildered barista, and then charged out into the night in hot pursuit of her nemesis. The shoulder-angel sighed. "Maybe I should've gone with a different moral. Oh well. C'est la vie."

About the Author

Well, you already know my name, since you've got this far into the book. As for other biographical data, I'm currently a third-year law student from Southern Indiana, and I work in a law library. Writing is my outlet from the pressures of legal studies, although sometimes the two do intermingle, as you might have noticed from Catrina's riveting discussion on the Fifth Amendment.

I have a blog, hypotheticallywriting.wordpress.com, in which I write the Catrina Chronicles, a series of episodic adventures in which Catrina attempts to save reality from being destroyed by Susan. I also write other short stories ranging from superhero fiction to sci-fi, such as my current series involving a girl named Rain who's trying not to be sacrificed to a volcano.

If you'd like to read other things I've written, you can go on the blog to find the Catrina Chronicles or the Volcano Rain series, or you can go on Amazon, where you will find Catrina in Space, a novel about Catrina's escapades with the space hamsters of the ship Dangling Participle, as they battle Susan and Murphy the Terrible.

Finally, on a personal note, I have a dream. My dream is to one day sell 423 copies of a novel I've written. Why 423, you ask? Because it's exactly one more than John Cusack's character sold of his fictional novel in the movie *2012*. His novel was about a space shuttle and Wisconsin, if I recall correctly. It seems like a good thing to shoot for.

Made in the USA
Charleston, SC
19 July 2013